ACTS OF MERCY

By Bill Pronzini and Barry N. Malzberg

The Running of Beasts
Night Screams
Prose Bowl

ACTS OF MERCY

Bill Pronzini
&
Barry N. Malzberg

SPEAKING VOLUMES, LLC

NAPLES, FLORIDA

2011

ACTS OF MERCY

ISBN 978-1-61232-127-1

For Bruni and Joyce
&
For Clyde Taylor

No one can examine the character of the American presidency without being impressed by its many-sidedness. The range of the President's functions is enormous. He is ceremonial head of state. He is a vital source of legislative suggestion. He is the final source of all executive decision. He is the authoritative exponent of the nation's foreign policy. To combine all these with the continuous need to be at once the representative man of the nation and the leader of his political party is clearly a call upon the energies of a single man unsurpassed by the exigencies of any other political office in the world.

—Harold J. Laski
The American Presidency

Being a President is like riding a tiger. A man has to keep on riding or be swallowed.

—Harry S. Truman

ACTS OF MERCY

Prologue

Do you want to check over these appointments, Mrs. Augustine?

Not particularly. Oh all right, Elizabeth, let me see them. Yes, yes. What about this United Jewish Appeal luncheon tomorrow? Do you think I really have to attend?

How can I tell you that, Mrs. Augustine?

I suppose you can't, can you. It's just that there are so many decisions to make and it would be nice to have someone help me make a few of them. The small ones, at least.

I understand.

Do you? Then give me your opinion on the UJA luncheon. Should I attend?

Well, yes, I believe you should. It was scheduled three months ago, remember. And after the President's press conference this morning, it might create the wrong impression if the First Lady were to cancel out.

You're right, of course. Elizabeth?

Yes, Mrs. Augustine?

About the press conference. What did you think of the President's remarks on Israel?

Oh, well, I'm sure he didn't mean them as they were interpreted by the press.

Certainly he didn't. It's just that he's been under a terrible strain recently. We've all been under a terrible strain these past few months.

Yes, I know.

Why do you say it like that?.So gravely, with that troubled look in your eyes.

I'm not troubled, Mrs. Augustine.

But you are. You've been my confidential secretary for a long time; I know you fairly well. Something is bothering you.

It's ... nothing I can explain, exactly.

I'd like you to try.

Well, it's just a feeling that something is ... wrong here in the White House.

Wrong?

Yes. It's like an undercurrent, a feeling of ... oh, this sounds melodramatic, but a feeling of strangeness, of impending tragedy.

Tragedy? What sort of tragedy?

I don't know, Mrs. Augustine.

Does it involve the President?

I'm not sure. I suppose it must, in some way.

Nothing is going to happen to the President, Elizabeth.

Oh, I didn't mean to say that. Of course nothing is going to happen to him.

Is there anything specific that makes you feel the way you do?

No, nothing specific. I guess I just wish ...

What? What do you wish?

That everything was the way it was up until six months ago. That the media hadn't turned against the President, that so many things hadn't been going wrong and the administration wasn't under so much pressure. That Peter Kineen and his people weren't trying to split the party again, the way it was four years ago. Maybe it's all of those things that make me feel so ... uneasy.

Yes. Maybe it is.

Are you all right, Mrs. Augustine? You look a little pale.

I'm just tired, Elizabeth. All this talk about strangeness and tragedy—it's enough to unnerve anyone.

I'm sorry, Mrs. Augustine. But you insisted that I tell you what was on my mind.

Yes. I did, didn't I?

If you don't feel well, we could cancel the UJA luncheon today. And I could call Doctor Whiting—

No. I don't want to see Doctor Whiting. I'm fine; I'll go to the luncheon as scheduled.

Do you want to dictate any letters this morning?

No. You can leave now, Elizabeth. I'll call you if I need you.

Just as you say, Mrs. Augustine. And I'm sorry again if I upset you; I won't say anything more about my foolish intuitions. Everything will be all right, I know that.

Of course it will. Everything will be fine.

Tragedy. My God. But she's wrong, there won't be any tragedy. Nothing is going to happen to Nicholas. Nothing is going to happen. Nothing is going to happen.

Monday, May 14

The Honorable Nicholas Franklin Augustine
President of the United States
The White House
1600 Pennsylvania Avenue
Washington, D.C.

Dear Mr. President:

I urge you to take what I am about to say in the absolute seriousness with which it is written.

Despite the necessary anonymity of this letter, I am not a crank. On the contrary I am someone quite close to you, personally and politically—a member of the inmost White House circle. But for reasons which will become clear, I cannot at this time tell you who I am. I must call no more attention to myself than I already gain as a result of my position.

The tragic realities of the situation are these, Mr. President. Not everyone you trust is as faithful to you as I am. There are those among your staff who are deceitful, who care only for the furtherance of their own positions and not at all for you or for the common good of the country, that same good to which you yourself have been selflessly dedicated since your inauguration. These individuals believe you to be weak and ineffectual, and they have formed a treacherous alliance against you. They are doing everything within their power to undermine your credibility so that you will be defeated for renomination in Saint Louis in July. Secretly, slyly, they have placed their support with the coalition headed by Peter Kineen.

In all good conscience I cannot at this time reveal the names of these turncoats, for I have no specific evidence against any one person. But I do have very strong suspicions, and it is only a matter of time until I am able to obtain proof.

But time may be another of your enemies, and that is why we are writing this letter. I mean, why I am writing this letter. You must be alert to the danger confronting you, Mr. President. You must be vigilant, as we are. As I

We take our fingers from the typewriter keys, cease their clattering; then we rip the letter from the carriage, tear it into tiny pieces and drop the pieces into the wastebasket. It is too painful for us to write in the first-person singular because we are not singular. Other people think we are, of course—as *I* thinks we are—but *we* know differently. This is both good and bad. It allows us to observe and to plan in emotionless privacy, but it also hinders our ability to function in what I would call a normal fashion.

The idea of writing a letter was a poor one in the first place, we know that now. If it was not ignored completely, it would plant seeds of doubt and unease of the wrong type: vigilance for the existence of a "paranoid crank," rather than vigilance for the true danger.

No, we must have more knowledge before we can take action of any kind. And when we have that knowledge, the action we take must not be the writing of letters. Nor personal appeals or any other sort of passive endeavor. We are beginning to understand that the strongest of measures are called for, and that we alone must carry them out. Only then can the threat to Nicholas Augustine be neutralized.

And we are beginning to understand too, as we sit here

alone in this quiet room, what those measures must be. After all, as has been demonstrated throughout history, there is only one just way to deal with traitors.

They must be executed.

PART ONE
The Capitol

One

When Christopher Justice entered the Oval Office, Nicholas Augustine was standing at the French doors behind his
desk, staring out at the White House grounds. He turned as
Justice approached, gave him a wan smile. "Sit down,
Christopher," he said.

"Yes sir."

Justice sat on one of the leather chairs facing the desk,
buttocks resting on only half of the cushion, feet planted
firmly. He felt vaguely ill at ease, as he always did when the
President summoned him here. There was something about
the Oval Office that instilled a sense of awe and humility in
him: the great men who had occupied these premises, the
momentous decisions that had been made here, the heads of
state who had maybe sat on this very same chair. He put his
hands flat on his knees, waiting quietly.

Augustine remained standing before the French doors,
framed between the American flag and the blue-and-white
President's flag, backlit by the wash of hot May sunlight
coming through the scrubbed glass. To Justice the President

looked imposing in that aspect, larger than life. But then Augustine came forward in heavy movements and sat at the desk, and the illusion vanished and he was just a handsome man in his mid-fifties—cool, sharply drawn features, fine cheekbones, gentle gray eyes. A weary man, too, Justice thought. You could see that in the faint slump of his shoulders, in the crosshatched lines under the eyes and around the wide mouth, in the distracted motions of his hands as he began straightening the clutter of papers in front of him.

"Well, Christopher," the President said finally, "I suppose you've read this morning's papers."

"Yes sir, I've read them."

"Do you think my comments at the press conference yesterday were anti-Semitic?"

"No sir, of course not."

"Of course not," Augustine agreed, and there was heat in his deep baritone voice. "I said, quote, Israel's decision to conduct their first atomic experiments on the Sinai is as regrettable as Egypt's similar decision, and I am distressed by the automatic trend of American foreign policy to support Israel in any dispute between that nation and other Middle Eastern powers. It permits us potentially to be held hostage to another's rather arbitrary actions. In the event of conflict I would not commit this administration at this time to the defense of Israel or *any* Middle Eastern nation. Unquote. If that is an anti-Semitic statement I'm a steam locomotive."

The President shook his head, ran a hand over a fan of cables. "These are communications from the distinguished secretary of state. *He* thinks I made a dangerous error, but that he might be able to save the situation. That's how he puts it in one of these cables: 'I might be able to save the situation.' Oberdorfer, you know, can be a horse's ass without half-trying."

Justice began to feel uncomfortable. He was, after all,

only a Secret Service bodyguard; he was not sure it was proper for Augustine to be talking to him so candidly about issues and personalities. But more and more of late the President had taken to summoning him for brief, off-the-cuff discussions that had become increasingly confidential. Justice was flattered that the President would choose him as a confidante, but he simply did not feel qualified to share the more intimate details of political life.

Augustine plucked a folded section of the Washington *Post* from under a pile of folders. "The editorial in here is damned near libelous," he said. "Did you see it, Christopher?"

"I skimmed it, yes sir."

"They not only infer that I'm a racist, they say I've been ignoring foreign policy, implementing superficial domestic programs, and spending too much time at The Hollows. They say I'm retreating from responsibility and insulating myself from the realities of my office." Irritably the President tossed the paper into his wastebasket. "They want us to believe those are the sentiments of the American people. Well I don't believe it for a minute."

"Neither do I, sir," Justice said.

The President fell silent again, staring down at the desk top. The desk was massive, six feet long and four feet wide, made from the timbers of a British sailing barque, a present from Queen Victoria to President Rutherford B. Hayes in 1879—the same desk President Kennedy and then President Carter had used. On one corner of it was a small O-scale brass model of a locomotive, one of several of his collection of railroad items that adorned the office; Augustine lifted it, looked at it for a long moment, put it down again and picked up a gold-framed photograph of the First Lady taken at the White House Inaugural Ball.

At length he sighed, set the photograph down carefully, and said in a perfunctory way, "I wonder if those media bastards understand what it's really like for a man in my position, how *alone* it makes you feel sometimes. I wonder if anyone understands that except my predecessors in this office."

"I think I have an idea, sir," Justice said.

The President looked across at him again with interest. "Do you really?"

"I think so."

"Maybe you do, at that," Augustine said. "You're so supportive, Christopher. I've noticed that before, though I suppose I marked it down to the nature of your job. But it's more than that, isn't it."

"I'm not sure I know what you mean, sir."

"How old are you?"

"Thirty-nine."

"I can remember when I was thirty-nine," the President said. "I was a lot like you are now. A simple man, a man of the people. But that's all changed." He paused speculatively. "Maybe you'd be a better person to sit in this chair than I am."

Justice blinked. "I, sir?"

"Yes. A young man, self-contained, in tune with the needs of the people. And what a magnificent name for a President—Justice! Have you ever been politically ambitious, Christopher?"

"No sir. I'm qualified to be a police officer, that's all."

"And you're proud of your position, proud to serve your country in this capacity."

"Yes sir, I am."

"You'd give your life for me, if it came to that."

"You know I would, Mr. President."

"That doesn't seem just, now does it?" Augustine said. "Why should one common man die for another, eh?"

"Because if somebody like me dies, the world doesn't lose much," Justice said. "But you're a great leader, the world needs you—"

"Does it?" Augustine said. "I wonder."

Justice could not think of anything appropriate to say; he looked down at his hands. It grew quiet in the office, and when he glanced up again, the President's head was bowed and he was wearily massaging his temples. Justice felt compassion stir inside him. It wasn't fair what the media was doing to Nicholas Augustine, he thought; in fact, it was almost criminal.

Four years ago Augustine had risen from relative anonymity as junior senator from California to rally a party so badly split that it was given no hope of succeeding to power. When he had captured public favor with his low-key and old-fashioned campaign and won the election by an amazing four million popular votes, the press had been for the most part quietly supportive. And they had remained that way during the first half of his term. Only then relations had weakened with Russia and China, and energy and other important domestic policies had failed to be implemented, and the jobless rate had soared, and the media had finally turned on Augustine, had begun to criticize him with increasing vehemence as a weak, ineffectual leader, as an overly simplistic man with a superficial grasp of issues. As a result, the President's popularity—over sixty percent for nearly the first three years—had begun to dip sharply during the past six months. Now, anything he did or said was subject to controversy, misinterpretation, and attack from all sides; even members of his own party, led by maverick Kentucky senator Peter Kineen, had opened another split and were vowing to keep Augustine from seeking a second term by wresting the nomination away from him at the forthcoming convention in Saint Louis.

It was terrible to see, Justice thought, what this constant pressure was doing to the President. He believed Nicholas Augustine had been and still was a strong leader. The world was at peace, the inflation rate had remained in a steady decline, the administration had been totally open and honest in every respect, and if no important domestic policies were being implemented, it was the fault of a hostile Congress. Augustine had made mistakes, yes—but was there ever a President who had not made mistakes? The ills of the country and of the world could not be laid to him; he had done all he could, and had tried to do more, and that was all anyone could expect of any President.

Justice said quietly, "Should I leave you alone now, sir?"

Augustine lowered his hands. "Yes," he said, "maybe you should. I have an appointment with Mr. Harper in a few minutes and there are some papers I should look over before he gets here."

Justice stood and nodded respectfully and went out of the office, past George Radebaugh, the appointments secretary, who did not look up from his desk, and into the outer corridor. The image of the President's strained face hung heavily in his mind.

Two

In the executive restroom down the hall from the Oval Office, Maxwell Harper was drying his hands on a towel when the door opened and the President's favorite bodyguard stepped inside. He turned as the man, Justice, said, "Oh, good morning, Mr. Harper."

"Justice."

Harper watched him cross to one of the urinals, stand there in a stiff, almost military posture of attention. He wondered with dry humor if the Secret Service indoctrinated its men to urinate that way. They were a regimented lot, in any case, and while Harper felt little common ground with any of them—they were like bland sticks of furniture: necessary, functional, unobtrusive—he admitted to an admiration for their unshakable control. He was a controlled man himself; he believed that absolute control, at all times, in all circumstances, was the key to success. It had been the key to his own success, certainly: his rise from political science professor at Harvard to the Wilson chair at Northwestern to Nicholas Augustine's foremost advisor on domestic affairs.

When Justice had finished at the urinal he came over to the row of washbasins, one removed from where Harper stood, and began to soap his hands. Harper studied him as he replaced the towel on its rack. Nondescript; average height, average weight, brown hair and brown eyes, no distinguishing features or marks. A cipher in every respect. He knew that the President had been spending a considerable amount of time with the man lately, discussing God knew what as if they were intimate friends, and he wished he understood what it was about Justice that inspired this confidence. That fawning deference of his, perhaps; Augustine had always had a weakness for people who told him he was right, strong, a great leader.

Harper said, "Have you talked to the President this morning, Justice?"

Justice straightened, as if coming to attention. "Yes sir," he said. Colorless voice, too, full of servility. "I just left the Oval Office."

"Did he say anything about the press conference yesterday?"

"Well, he feels people misunderstood his remark on Israel."

"Of course. Which is exactly why he should not have made it."

"Sir?"

"Suppose you were a Jew," Harper said. "How would you feel about the President today?"

"I'm not a Jew, Mr. Harper."

"Do you know any Jews?"

"Yes sir."

"Have you talked to any of them this morning?"

"No sir."

"Maybe you should, Justice. Maybe you should."

Harper caught up his briefcase and went to the door. As he turned the knob he glanced back at Justice, saw him standing before the basin and frowning slightly into the mirror. An odd feeling of satisfaction touched Harper; he nodded once at Justice's reflection and then opened the door and went out.

The President was on the telephone in the Oval Office; he waved Harper to one of the chairs before his desk. Harper took the closest of them, moving it so that it paralleled to the right corner, and listened for a moment to what Augustine was saying into the receiver. But it was nothing of significance: he was talking to Austin Briggs, the press secretary, about dinner that night, telling him to issue invitations to Attorney General and Mrs. Wexford and to congressional liaison Ed Dougherty.

Waiting, Harper noticed that the lines in Augustine's face were deeply etched, that the skin of his neck had a loose, wattled appearance. He recalled his own image in the restroom mirror: carefully trimmed black mustache; romanesque nose, shrewd gray eyes, clear and unlined skin. We're the same age, he thought, but he looks sixty-five and I look forty-five. He's an old man, he's grown into an old man.

Harper shifted his gaze to the desk, felt a faint distaste at the disorganized spread of papers there. The framed photograph of the First Lady in her inaugural gown caught his attention then, and in spite of himself he let his eyes linger on it. She was one of the most beautiful and alluring women he had ever known; even in that photograph she radiated an aura of restrained sensuality that was unmistakable. Forty-two years old now—and married to a fifty-six-year-old man who looked sixty-five and who was starting to flounder in office, perhaps seriously. Was Augustine starting to flounder elsewhere as well, in his private relations with Claire ... ?

Harper dug his nails into his palms, pulled his head away from the photograph. Claire Augustine was the wife of the

President; it was indecent, and foolish and pointless, to think of her in any sort of intimate way. Strict control; at all times, in all circumstances, strict control.

Augustine finally said good-bye to Briggs and replaced the telephone handset. Then he reached across the desk for one of a dozen pipes in a circular rack, put it between his teeth without filling it, and immediately picked up and began fondling one of the railroad collectibles that cluttered his desk and the office. Railroadiana, Augustine called them. Harper had always considered the President's passion for trains to be a childish and undignified hobby; but then, that same passion had apparently endeared him to the electorate during his campaign for the presidency. It was generally conceded among political experts that Augustine's use of his privately owned train, the California Special (since re-dubbed the Presidential Special, of course) to conduct an anachronistic cross-country whistle-stop campaign, the first national politician to do so since Harry Truman in 1948, had won him as many grass-roots votes as his "New America" platform.

"All right, Maxwell," the President said at length, "I suppose you're going to jump on me like everybody else."

"I have no intention of jumping on you," Harper said. "I think you made a mistake yesterday and I think you had better take steps to rectify it, but that's all I'm going to say. My area of expertise, after all, is domestic affairs."

"So it is."

"Did you read those briefs?"

"Briefs?" Augustine replaced the railroad collectible and folded his hands in front of him. "You mean the Indian situation in Montana?"

"Of course that's what I mean."

"I glanced at them, yes."

"Glanced at them? Nicholas, this is a serious domestic issue," Harper said, and he could not quite keep the exasperation out of his voice. "And in less than an hour you have a meeting with Governor Hendricks and Walter Sandcrane and Leo Wade from the Bureau of Indian Affairs."

"Sandcrane? Oh yes, the Indian spokesman. Well, don't worry about it, Maxwell. I can handle the arbitration. There won't be any Indian takeover of the Crow reservations in Montana."

"Cheyenne," Harper said. "For God's sake, it's the Cheyenne who are threatening to take over their reservations."

"All right, yes, the Cheyenne." Augustine leaned back, closed his eyes for a moment, opened them again. "Do you have any idea how tired I am, Maxwell? How tired I really am?"

"We're all tired these days," Harper said. "But that doesn't excuse a lack of preparation or errors in diplomacy."

"Meaning Israel or the Indian problem?"

"Both, as a matter of fact."

"I told you, I'll handle things."

Harper was silent.

"But then I've got to have a rest," Augustine said, "even if it's only for a few days. What I think we'll do is go out to The Hollows at the end of the week. On Sunday."

"Again? We were just out there ten days ago—"

"I know that, don't you think I know that?"

"Nicholas, the media is already accusing you of spending a disproportionate amount of time in California. The *Post* editorial this morning—"

"To hell with the *Post*. The Western White House is the only place I can relax, you know that."

"I wish you wouldn't call The Hollows the Western White House," Harper said. "It's the same phrase Nixon used for San Clemente, as the press has been so fond of pointing out."

Augustine made an impatient gesture. "It's my ranch and

I'll call it any damned thing I please. The point is, I need another few days of relaxation, Maxwell; I *need* them. We're going to The Hollows on Sunday and that's all there is to it."

Harper just looked at him. The Hollows again, he thought. Only a few days this time. Again. This time . . .

Three

Nicholas Augustine sipped wine from his crystal goblet and looked around the table and wished fervently that he and Claire had decided to dine alone tonight. The evening had begun amiably enough with cocktails in the Green Room, but once they had all come in here to the State Dining Room for dinner, conversation had inevitably gotten around to Israel. It was Briggs who had brought up the subject, over the consommé, and of course Wexford had had to have his say over the salad; only Dougherty and Claire's secretary, Elizabeth Miller, had remained silent on the topic, although it was apparent how the two of them felt. By the time the chateaubriand was served, silence had mercifully resettled—but Augustine had long since lost his appetite for anything except the wine.

A damned shame too, because he liked chateaubriand. He even liked the State Dining Room, with its restful green colors and its oak paneling. Claire preferred to eat here instead of in the Family Dining Room, which was why they had company for dinner most evenings; it would hardly have been appropriate, she said, for them to dine here alone. But if they *had* dined alone, damn it, he might have been able to enjoy his meal and to unwind a bit, instead of suffering a fresh onslaught of aggravation.

Why wouldn't they leave him alone, all of them, for just a little while?

Out of the tail of his eye he saw the huge portrait of Abraham Lincoln that hung over the fireplace, and he smiled wryly. You and me, Abe, he thought, and raised his glass in a small silent toast.

He took another sip of wine and put the goblet down; but as he did so it struck the edge of his plate, making a sharp ringing sound that cut heavily into the silence. Everyone looked at him as though he had rapped for attention—Claire, Austin Briggs, Julius Wexford, Ed Dougherty, Elizabeth Miller, and Wexford's gray little wife Rachel. Rachel blinked at him like a startled bird; her eyes were as gray as her hair, as her complexion, and the white evening gown she wore only served to complete the colorless study. In contrast, even Elizabeth, an angular brunette in her middle thirties, wearing a dark blue gown and a pair of gold-rimmed glasses that gave her a properly secretarial air, seemed attractive. And Claire, Augustine noted with some pride, looked even more stunning than usual: blonde hair done up with a jeweled comb, china-blue eyes alert and inquisitive, skin so smooth it seemed translucent; gracious and poised as always, although she seemed somewhat subdued tonight. Her dress was blue-green, the same color as her eyes, and it seemed to flow against her when she moved, like seawater.

She said, "Yes, Nicholas?"

Well, Augustine thought, I might as well have my say too; Briggs had the consommé, Wexford had the salad, and I'd better take the chateaubriand before Dougherty does. The evening is ruined anyway. As if there had been no five-minute lull in the conversation, he said, "Have any of you heard the story about the old Jew, filled with poverty and misfortune, who one day shakes his fist at the heavens and says, 'God, I know we're Your chosen people, but will You please, for Your own sake, choose someone else.' "

Rachel Wexford made a small choking sound, covered her mouth with a napkin. Wexford scowled and patted her hand. Dougherty and Elizabeth looked at each other and then down at their wine goblets. Briggs opened his mouth, closed it, opened it again, and finally put a forkful of potato inside it. Claire watched him steadily, neither surprised nor shocked, merely attentive.

Augustine said, "No? Well how about the one where the two old Jews—old enemies who have hated each other for forty years—meet on a railroad platform in Czarist Russia?" He finished his wine. "These two old Jews, you see, hadn't spoken to each other for years, but finally one of them is unable to hold his silence and he says to the other, 'Moshe, where are you going on this fine day?' And Moshe, you understand, is a stubborn man, he doesn't want to give his old enemy the satisfaction of a quick answer; so he considers for a time and then he says, 'Well, Schmuel, to tell you the truth, which is more than you deserve, I am going this fine day to the province of Minsk.' Schmuel looks at him then, shrewdly, and he says, 'I know what you are, Moshe; you are a liar whose word can never be trusted; you would betray me at every opportunity. You hope to deceive me into thinking you are really going to the province of Pinsk, but I know you so well that the truth is, you are obviously going to Minsk after all.' "

Augustine burst out laughing. None of the others joined in, although Claire seemed to smile faintly; they continued to stare at him.

"Do you understand?" Augustine said. "Schmuel says, 'You think I am to believe you are not going to Minsk, where you say you're going, but to Pinsk, but I know you lie so you must really be going to Minsk.' "

Silence.

Augustine shrugged. "I believe I'll have a little more wine," he said, and motioned to Edmund, the staff waiter, who was standing quietly to one side. Edmund approached and poured more beaujolais into Augustine's glass.

Briggs said stiffly, "Mr. President, I hope you don't intend to tell either of those stories *publicly* . . ."

"Oh, for God's sake, Austin, they're jokes. Wry comments on the nature of the Hebraic mind."

"And very funny, I'm sure," Rachel Wexford said.

Augustine thought: Christ, she's a twit.

Wexford wiped his hands carefully on his napkin, put the napkin down, and took a long, careful sip of water. He was a heavyset man, florid, jowly, wearing a dark suit with a patterned red tie; his face had taken on more color, so that it seemed now to have achieved a hue remarkably similar to that of the beaujolais. The two of them, Julius and Rachel, made quite a pair, Augustine thought. One of them gray, one of them red.

Wexford said, "Well I hardly think either story is funny, Mr. President. They seem more like racial slurs—"

"They are not racial slurs," Augustine said. "Why does anybody who tells an ethnic joke automatically become guilty of a racial slur? And by extension, of bigotry?"

"The Jewish people are very important to us," Wexford said sententiously. He took a cigar from his coat pocket, rolled it between his fingers, and then put it away again when his wife frowned at him. "In terms of the demographics of the vote, and because they contribute disproportionately well to their actual percentage of the population—"

"I am *not* demeaning the Jews," Augustine said. He was beginning to lose his temper. "I fully understand their political importance, Julius, *and* their racial importance, and the public record makes it clear that I am not an anti-Semite. I'm only trying to make a damned point here—"

Claire reached across to touch his hand with cool fingers. "I think you've made it, Nicholas," she said quietly. "Don't get yourself upset."

"I'm not upset," Augustine said, and put his hand on top of hers, squeezed it briefly and then pushed it away. "Damn it, what's wrong with a little honesty? A few years back Moynihan made a comment about 'benign neglect' where blacks are concerned, and right away people twisted his words into something totally alien to what he meant. That is exactly what is happening to me right now: I'm being convicted of a crime I didn't commit on the basis of semantics. The truth is, what I said in yesterday's press conference is absolutely defensible."

"Anything is defensible, Mr. President," Dougherty said. He was a thin deliberate man in his early forties, like Briggs a bachelor, though not for much longer if Elizabeth Miller had her way: they had been keeping steady company for the past year. "But certain defenses create more complications than others."

"Yes," Briggs agreed, "and with the convention only two months ahead at that."

"History has a way of accelerating nowadays," Elizabeth said. "This will all be forgotten news by the time we convene in Saint Louis."

"Will it?" Wexford shook his head. "I doubt it."

"What do you think I ought to do then, Julius?" Augustine asked with forced calm.

"What I said earlier. Call a meeting with members of the Jewish community—the senators from New York and Connecticut, the heads of B'nai B'rith and the Council of Rabbis and the United Jewish Appeal. Issue a clarification."

"There's nothing to clarify, how many times do I have to tell you that? Any so-called clarification is going to look defensive, as if we're conceding fault. We'd lose all respect—all self-respect."

Briggs said, "We've got to have something to give to the press. They've been relentless, and all I've had to say to them are no-comments or referrals to previous statements. I'm beginning to feel a little like Ron Ziegler and I can't say I like that very much."

Augustine looked at him with increasing dislike. Young (thirty-seven, wasn't it?), boyish-looking with his overlong hair and his freckles, glib most of the time, but with a nasty penchant for whining in moments of stress; the kind of man who, if he had been on a derailed train, would have rushed to save himself first and to hell with everyone else. Augustine wondered what the hell possessed him to give Briggs the press secretary's job in the first place.

As if interpreting his thoughts, Claire said to Briggs, "If you don't like your position, Austin, you can always resign." Her voice was soft, pleasant, but there was an undercurrent of toughness in it that Augustine knew well.

Briggs seemed taken aback. "Excuse me?" he said.

"After all, Austin," she said, "you don't have to run the Presidential press office if you'd rather not. You could certainly go back to work for the Los Angeles *Times,* if that's what you'd prefer, and the deputy press secretary could assume your duties. I'm sure Frank Tanaguchi would be delighted at the promotion."

Briggs blushed, coughed, and lowered his gaze to his water glass; he had been put in his place and he was intelligent enough to realize it.

Claire turned to look at Augustine, a long, searching look that seemed to have some meaning he could not quite grasp. Then she smiled and said, "Now I think this discussion has gone far enough for one evening. This is supposed to be a quiet dinner party, not a shouting match. Why don't all of you sleep on the matter and discuss it again tomorrow?"

The anger inside Augustine faded. Claire had always had a calming effect on him. She was a strong woman; sometimes he thought she was stronger than he was, and more stable, and more perceptive. Sometimes she intimidated him just a little, because he never knew exactly what was going on inside her head, while she always seemed to know what was going on inside his.

He said, "I suppose you're right."

Wexford nodded reluctantly, and Ed Dougherty said, "Yes, we might as well table it."

"Fine," Claire said. "Then we'll have coffee and dessert. Edmund."

But she kept on looking at Augustine, and it was only after the table was cleared that she took her eyes from him and then leaned forward to say something cheerful about current fashions to Rachel Wexford. Who blinked and bobbed her head and kept her chin tucked against her thin breast.

And with sudden belated insight, Augustine understood the meaning in his wife's eyes, understood that it was not only Austin Briggs whom she had put in his place, but Augustine himself; that she had been telling *him* he did not have to run the presidency either if he would rather not. If you can't stand the heat, get out of the kitchen. . . .

Edmund brought in a cart bearing a silver coffee service and silver dishes of cake. Claire said, "Black Forest cherry cake, Nicholas—your favorite."

Augustine poured himself another glass of wine.

Four

Off-duty at six o'clock, Christopher Justice drove his three-year-old Ford sedan from the White House to George-town, ate a light supper in a sidewalk café on M Street, and then strolled to Thirty-first Street, where there were several new and used bookstores that stayed open in the evenings. It was a hot night and the tree-shaded streets were crowded, but in the bookstores it was cool and quiet—particularly in the basement of O'Hare's, an antiquarian bookseller who maintained a substantial and dusty stock of hardcover and paperback mysteries.

Reading and collecting mystery novels was Justice's one and only hobby. He enjoyed fishing and an occasional game of tennis, but by nature he was a solitary man who did not make friends easily; a member of the Secret Service staff, in any case, seldom had the opportunity for socializing. He was one of those men totally devoted to his job, taking his greatest pleasure as well as his sustenance from that work. And maybe that was the reason he had never married, never been seriously involved with any of the women he had known over the years.

He had gotten interested in mysteries while he was still on the Washington police force, and had begun collecting them on a small scale almost immediately. In his apartment in Alexandria—which he used only on his days off; when he was on duty he occupied a small room in the West Wing of the White House—he had several hundred editions of British and American crime novels. He especially liked the early English mysteries: they had a slow, measured pace; they were peopled with old colonels who had fought in India for British imperialism, and proper ladies and even more proper gentlemen, and eccentric detectives and exotic foreigners, and high-strung nieces and nephews who were interested in archeological excavations or inheritances from dead or dying relatives; they dealt with genteel puzzles and bloodless murders and polite investigative techniques. They were self-contained, mentally challenging, and far-removed from his own experiences, and they served him in the same way that the games of chess or bridge served other thoughtful policemen of one type or another.

Justice moved slowly, browsing, among the library-type stacks. On one of the "C" shelves he found a battered ex-library copy of Agatha Christie's *Murder on the Calais Coach,* third American edition, and took it down and opened it. He had developed an interest in trains since he had been assigned as the President's bodyguard and had had the opportunity to travel with Augustine on the Presidential Special between Los Angeles and The Hollows in Northern California; and *Murder on the Calais Coach,* with its fascinating Orient Express background, was one of the classic train mysteries. He had a paperback reissue of the book in Alexandria, but it had been a long time since he had read it. He decided he wanted to reread it and that he would buy this copy instead of driving across the Potomac for the soft-cover edition.

Tucking it under his arm, he continued to browse. The air in the bookstore was musty and comfortably moist, unlike the atmosphere of the White House which seemed always to be dry, the kind of air that could give someone a sinus condition; the familiar ambiance of old books was pleasant. And yet tonight he could not quite relax, could not seem to isolate himself, as he usually could in bookstores like O'Hare's, from the responsibilities of the presidency—responsibilities which were his own by inference and because of his duty.

The plain truth was, he was worried about the President.

Outwardly Augustine was the same sensible, forthright figure he had always been, but at the edges, Justice thought, he was beginning to weaken. Six months ago he would not have made those remarks on Israel, as essentially reasonable as they had been. They were politically damaging and upsetting to the influential Jewish electorate, as Maxwell Harper, in his superior fashion, had pointed out that morning. Six months ago the President had not been so bothered by attacks in the press. Hadn't he gone on national television several times to quietly and eloquently defend himself and his administration on controversial issues? Hadn't he laughed publicly at the disparaging comments in *Newsweek* about his "neurasthenic habit" of mumbling distractedly to himself from time to time, his "obsession with railroads" and his "adolescent predilection" for humming and sometimes informally singing folk ballads such as "John Henry" and "The Wreck of Old 98"?

Lost in thought now, Justice turned abruptly out of the stacks and climbed the stairs to the bookstore's street level. Six months ago the President had not seen fit to spend an average of ten days a month at The Hollows—nor, for that matter, had he found it necessary to unburden himself to a Secret Service bodyguard. Six months ago it had looked as though renomination and reelection were certainties; but now, with his popularity under forty-five percent in all the polls, not only the press but several prominent Washington political figures were saying that the Peter Kineen coalition would, after all, be able to take the nomination away from him in Saint Louis—

"Two dollars," the clerk at the front counter said.

"Excuse me?"

"This book. It's two dollars plus tax."

"Oh," Justice said, "sure." Embarrassed by his abstraction, he paid the man quickly and took the copy of *Murder on the Calais Coach* into the muggy night.

As he made his way through the crowds, past the sidewalk flower vendors and the sellers of beads and trinkets and leather goods, he thought about Peter Kineen. Kineen was a reactionary, considered by many to be a dangerous man: a latter-day Ronald Reagan. If he was able to wrest the nomination from Augustine in Saint Louis, the party might be in serious trouble. And the country would surely be in serious trouble, because even if Kineen lost the election, the minority-party candidate would almost certainly be Elton Kheel, the governor of Illinois, who was an old-line machine politician and who was reputed to be a closet hawk on foreign policy despite his avowals to the contrary.

Justice was hardly an expert on politics, but his close proximity to the President had given him a certain inside knowledge; it seemed obvious to him that the only hope for the future lay with Nicholas Augustine. Which meant that the President *had* to draw himself together, seal off vulnerability, rally the party around him as he had done four years ago.

And he will, Justice told himself. You had to have faith, that was all.

You had to have faith.

Five

Claire was lying on her back in the canopied rosewood bed, the covers pulled up to her breasts and her hands resting palms up at her sides, when Nicholas Augustine came through the door that connected their two bedrooms. It was dark in the room, except for a pale shaft of moonlight that filtered through the south window and lay across the edge of the bed at her feet, as though it had prostrated itself there. Her eyes were closed, but Augustine could not tell if she was asleep.

He hesitated, holding the edge of the door with his left hand. But then she stirred, turned her head and opened her eyes. "Nicholas?" she said.

"Did I wake you?"

"No, I was just resting. Couldn't you sleep?"

"No. I have a hell of a headache." He rubbed his temples with the heels of both hands. "I suppose I drank too much wine at dinner."

"I suppose you did," she said mildly. "Did you want to join me?"

"Would you mind?"

"Of course not."

Augustine crossed the room, shed his bathrobe, and moved in beside her. The sheets were warm from her body, scented with the musky fragrance of her perfume, and when she laid her hip against his he felt desire move through him. But he lay quietly, looking up at the quilted underside of the canopy; she was a very desirable woman and he wanted her, and yet his mind was so full of political matters that he could not focus on the physical need.

She turned onto her side so that her breast flattened along his rib cage, reached up to touch his temples with her cool fingers. Massaging them gently in small circles, she asked. "Does this help?"

"A bit," Augustine said. *Wexford, Oberdorfer, Maxwell Harper, Israel, the Indian problem in Montana and the meeting with Wade and Hendricks and Sandcrane that had not gone at all well this afternoon ....* "A little bit."

Seconds passed, a minute or two. Then Claire began to rub her thigh against his beneath the silk of her nightgown, in the same gentle rhythm, and he felt the need climbing within him, felt himself starting to respond. One of her hands lowered to open the buttons on his pajama top, to stroke his chest, and he rolled over to her then, and kissed her, and drew the straps of her gown away to release her breasts to his hands and then to his lips.

"Yes, dear," she said, "that's nice."

But he did not have a full erection; even her touch did not give it to him. *Israel, the Indians, the convention in Saint Louis ...* stop thinking! A little desperately, he tried to force himself to concentrate on the softness of her body, on the movements of her hands and of his own. Nothing happened. So he concentrated on himself, willing an erection, mind pleading with body—but that had even less effect, you could not begin to make love by focusing on yourself. Sex was two people, equal partners seeking to become one—

Claire said, "It'll happen, dear, it'll happen," and guided him to her. But she was not ready, her vulva was dry, the body as always telling truths that the spirit would deny, and he felt the last of his rigidity slip away. Damn it, damn it! Angry with himself, dismayed, he pushed away from her and lay on his back again, staring up at the canopy, listening to the dry rasp of his breathing. Beside him Claire made a soft sound in her throat that might have meant anything or nothing at all.

This was the sixth time in succession and the fifteenth or twentieth time in three months that he had failed her, failed himself. For years he had been able to keep this part of his life wholly segregated, unaffected by political pressures; now he seemed to have lost that ability. Impotent, he thought, and the word lay bitter and ugly in his mind. Where did all the power go: the potency, the strength? He was the same man he had always been, and yet things kept happening that intimated he might not be.

Maybe he should see Doctor Whiting, his personal and now the White House physician. But Whiting was a somewhat supercilious little man who thought exercise and a proper diet were the answers to most medical problems and that mental strain could better be relieved by positive thinking than by any medicinal aids. No, there was nothing Whiting could do—and he would have been embarrassed discussing impotency with him in any case. What he needed more than anything was another few days at The Hollows— to be home again in California, to lie with Claire in the big brass bed with the springs that could sing like train wheels in the night . . .

He realized that she had moved to him again; she caught his hand in hers. "Is there anything you want me to do, dear?"

"No," Augustine said, "it's just not going to work tonight." He felt irritable; his headache was worse now. He drew his hand away. "You're disappointed in me, aren't you."

"Of course not—"

"You don't have to pretend, Claire. You *are* disappointed in me, and not just because of what didn't happen a minute ago."

"I don't know what you mean."

"Don't you? I saw the look you gave me at dinner, after you put Austin in his place. You were telling me the same thing you told him, that maybe *I* ought to get out because I can't handle the presidency anymore."

She was silent for a time. "Yes," she said finally, "you're right that I don't think you should run for reelection. But it's not because I believe you can't handle the presidency. It's because of what the office is doing to you. Do you honestly feel you can go through another exhausting campaign, another four years without ..."

She broke off.

"Without what?" Augustine said.

"Without suffering any more. Without ruining your health. You've changed in these last few months, Nicholas. You've ... changed."

The irritability increased. "You're like all the rest of them," he said. "Pushing me with one hand and pulling me with the other. You all want something and when you can't have it or you've got it and you're afraid of losing it, you put the blame on me."

"Have I ever said or done anything in the twenty years we've been married that wasn't in your best interests?"

Her voice was soft, patient, reasonable; she was always so imperturbable, so in command of her emotions that at times like this it made him feel frustrated, inadequate. "What about *your* best interests?" he said. "I suppose you had no ambitions of your own, you never wanted to be the First Lady, the wife of the President of the United States."

"I wanted to be the wife of President Nicholas Augustine, yes. But you've given four important, productive years; isn't that enough work and sacrifice for one person? You're not a machine, Nicholas. You're a fifty-six-year-old man who—"

"Who is starting to lose his grip?"

"—who deserves a rest and a chance to live the remainder of his life in peace and privacy. It's not as if you would be leaving politics altogether; you would still have influence, you could—"

"I've heard enough of this," Augustine said. He swung out of bed, caught up his bathrobe.

"Nicholas . . ."

"Good night, Claire," he said, and walked out and shut the connecting door behind him.

Alone in his own bed, head throbbing, mind working like an engine that coughed and stuttered and would not shut down, he found himself listening to the faint noises that houses make in the night. Harry Truman had once said that the White House cracked and popped all night long, and that you could imagine that old Jackson or Andy Johnson or some other ghost was walking. It was a nice prison, he said, but a prison nevertheless. No man in his right mind would want to come here of his own accord.

And maybe he was right, Augustine thought. Restoration hadn't changed the old place any; it was still a prison full of the ghosts of long-dead presidents, wandering through the vast halls, whispering to the man who now occupied the premises, telling him things that he could not hear and dared not listen to if he could. Telling him that one day he would join them and add his voice to theirs, because no matter what he did from now on he was one of them: the presidency was a life sentence, an eternal sentence, and there was no way he was ever going to get out.

Six

We are still not quite sure of the identities of the traitors, but the evidence is beginning to mount strongly against one man in particular. Is he the leader of the conspiracy among those close to the President, of the turncoats who hide behind the guise of friendship and trust? We are beginning to believe that he is.

We must have more conclusive evidence before we can act—but we sense it will not be long until this final damning proof is revealed to us, until he stands before us fully exposed. And when that time comes, we will act immediately and without compunction. The conspiracy must be stopped at all costs; the traitor must be eliminated.

But we must be careful too. The President's safety and the President's future are in our hands; we must carry out our mission not only with dispatch but with caution and premeditation. There are those who would not understand our methods, those who would try to prevent us from acting if they suspected our intention.

Soft, then. Soft and cunning.

Death to the traitor on cat's paws.

Seven

At precisely nine o'clock Wednesday morning, Maxwell Harper knocked on the door of the Oval Study upstairs and then opened it and stepped inside. The room was empty. His immediate reaction was one of annoyance; he had called the President an hour earlier to request a private appointment, and Augustine had told him to come here at nine instead of to the Oval Office, and if there was one thing Harper detested it was a lack of punctuality.

He crossed the room and sat in one of the leather armchairs before the fireplace, placing his briefcase carefully on the floor beside him. The drapes were drawn across the windows that looked out on the south lawn, and the room seemed dark, oppressively cluttered. Too much furniture, haphazardly arranged; and too much emphasis on trains. Augustine's collection of railroadiana—a dozen different types of switch-stand lanterns, locomotive headlamps, an early telegrapher's outfit, a ticket-validating machine, glass cases filled with brass baggage checks and advertising memorabilia and dime novels and popular fiction dealing with railroads—made it look more like an obscure museum than a White House study. Harper himself was a neat, fastidious man whose bachelor apartment near the French embassy was a model of functional conservatism; he had always felt out of place here.

As he waited, his annoyance modulated into determination. Things, he had decided, were approaching a serious crisis point: the Israel gaffe, Augustine's inattention to the Indian problem in Montana, his decision to run off still again to The Hollows were all danger signals not to be treated lightly. The President was backing himself into a political corner, and that did not bode well for the country or for anyone in his administration.

He was badly worn out, which was understandable because the man had worked like a demon for the past three and a half years; but that was a symptom, not an explanation. The fact was, it was not Augustine who was responsible for what was happening, it was those with whom he had surrounded himself in responsible, influential positions. Men such as Franz Oberdorfer, and perhaps Julius Wexford and Austin Briggs—men Harper had not approved of from the beginning. They had given the President poor advice or not enough advice, used him to further their own careers, even circumvented him entirely like that demagogue Oberdorfer; and Augustine, never a forceful leader, had begun to buckle under the pressure and the dissension.

This close to the convention, a wholesale firing of these people was impossible because it would completely undermine public faith in the President. What could be done, what *had* to be done, was to make Augustine realize both the danger and his own fallibility and then to take steps to rectify matters. Rifts with the press had to be sutured, a strong and vocal reelection campaign had to be implemented, concessions to the National Committee and to certain special-interest groups and to the Jewish electorate had to be made that would induce them to remain in the

President's corner. Then, after renomination and reelection, Oberdorfer and the others could be systematically replaced—

The door to the Monroe Room across the study opened, interrupting Harper's reverie, and he glanced up. But it was not the President who entered; it was the First Lady.

Harper rose immediately. "Good morning, Mrs. Augustine," he said.

She hesitated for a moment, looking at him, and then came slowly across the room. She wore a beige pantsuit that accentuated the slim lines of her body, and her hair was done in a casual ponytail tied with a blue velvet ribbon. Harper felt the palms of his hands turn moist; she never failed to have that effect on him.

"Good morning," she said, and stopped a half-dozen paces away from him. Her tone was cool and curiously dull, and he realized in the dim light that she looked as tired as the President: small lines beneath her eyes, a pinched look to the corners of her mouth. He wondered if she understood the seriousness of Augustine's position. Surely she did understand, as intelligent and perceptive as she had always been.

He said, "I had a nine o'clock appointment with the President, so I came straight up. I hope you don't mind."

"No, I don't mind ... Maxwell."

"He's ten minutes late," Harper said. "Do you know where he is?"

A loose strand of hair had fallen away from her temple and she brushed it back into place in that absent, caressing way some attractive women had, both conscious and unconscious of its sensuality. "He had a meeting at eight o'clock with the security affairs advisor," she said. "I imagine he'll be here shortly."

She seemed to want to say something else, but did not; Harper had the impression that she was vaguely ill at ease. She was usually so poised, so self-assured, and yet in his presence she was oddly subject to fluctuating moods. Sometimes she seemed cold and distant, as if she did not like or trust him completely; at other times she was open and friendly in a way that bordered on affection. It occurred to him now, as it had before, that she intuited his carefully concealed attraction for her and perhaps responded to it. That under different circumstances she might have been receptive to him as an intimate.

Or as a lover? he thought.

Pointless thinking, damn it. *Pointless.*

At length she said, "If you'll excuse me, I have some things to do."

"Of course, Mrs. Augustine."

Harper watched her walk across to the hallway door, the play of her hips beneath the suit pants. When she got there, she paused and looked back at him, as if she still wanted to say something more; but again she did not speak. And a moment later she was gone.

Frowning, he returned to the chair by the fireplace and sat down again. He wished he understood her better, what motivated her, what went on behind that dispassionate public facade. Did Augustine himself understand her? Did anyone? She was the President's wife, she had by everyone's testimony more to do with this administration than any First Lady since Mrs. Woodrow Wilson—and yet, could it be that she was not working with the President so much as using their collaboration as cover for some sort of personal cachet?

He could not quite shake the pervasive feeling that she was something more and something less than what she seemed to be.

Eight

The press secretary's office was down the hall from the West Wing Reception Room, and as Christopher Justice turned the corner toward it a few minutes past noon, on an errand for the President, two men just emerged from the office were walking shoulder to shoulder and talking animatedly. Even though they had their backs to Justice, he recognized them: Attorney General Wexford and Peter Kineen.

Justice paused, looking after them. There was probably some innocuous reason for them to be together, but it struck him as odd that Kineen, the President's bitter rival, should be here in the White House; that he should be so intimate with the attorney general, who was also chairman of the President's reelection campaign. And odd, too, that both men had been together with Austin Briggs (whom Justice didn't particularly like because he sometimes seemed to use questionable judgment in his comments to the press).

Thoughtfully, he continued to the press secretary's office. When he entered he saw that there was no one at the outer reception desk: Briggs's private secretary had evidently gone to lunch. The door to the inner office stood ajar, and Justice crossed to it and knocked and then pushed it inward.

Briggs was seated at his desk, and he had apparently been studying a sheaf of papers spread out in front of him; but now he blinked at Justice, swept the papers together hastily, put them into a manila folder and his hand on top of the folder as if guarding it. His expression, Justice saw with some surprise, was like that of a child caught at some sort of mischief.

"I'm sorry if I'm intruding, Mr. Briggs," Justice said. "But the President asked me to stop by."

"The *President* asked you—?"

"Yes sir. He's busy and he couldn't come himself. He's planning to go to California this weekend and he'd like you to cancel the press luncheon scheduled for next Monday. He'd also like you to prepare a media release saying that he intends to remain at The Hollows for from three to five days for private policy discussions with members of his staff."

Briggs seemed nervously flustered, uneasy; he ran a hand through his hair, ran his tongue over his lips, and reached for a cigarette from the pack in front of him. Though they were approximately the same age, he appeared very young to Justice—had seemed that way from the first moment they'd met. Maybe because there was a certain obvious immaturity in the man.

"I don't understand," Briggs said. "Is this some sort of joke?"

"Joke, sir?" Justice felt himself frowning. "Of course not. Why would you think it's a joke?"

Briggs cleared his throat. "Well, it's just that going to The Hollows again while the press is still in an uproar over the Israel remarks ... well, I'm not sure it's such a wise decision."

Justice said, "It's the President's decision, Mr. Briggs. If you'd like to call him later on ..."

"No," Briggs said, "no, that won't be necessary. All right, I ... I'll take care of the cancellation and the release." He got up jerkily, like a man struggling out of water, crushed his unlighted cigarette in the heavy White House ashtray on his desk, and caught up the folder and tucked it under his arm. And went out past Justice, leaving the door open, hurrying.

Justice stood for a moment, confused and bothered by the press secretary's curious behavior. What was in those papers he had been studying? Did they have something to do with the presence earlier of the attorney general and Senator Kineen? Was he up to something, and had he been guiltily worried that Justice would realize it and inform the President?

He hurried back to the Oval Office.

Nine

For Augustine it had been a typically grueling day.

To begin it there had been a seven A.M. conference with the national energy advisor to discuss several of his bottlenecked energy proposals. Then there had been a brief meeting with the chairman of the Council of Economic Advisors, followed by a meeting with the security affairs advisor on intelligence matters. Shortly past nine he had gone upstairs to the Oval Study for a brief and painful consultation with Maxwell Harper, who had not told him anything he didn't already know or suspect; but he was damned if he would listen to any more accusations that he was starting to make serious political blunders, and he had cut the meeting short.

At ten o'clock he'd met with members of the cabinet, minus Oberdorfer who was still in Tel Aviv, and Wexford whose absence was unexplained. Discussion of economic imperatives—going over the same ground he had covered with the economic council chairman—and then of the grave status of the French franc (during which he had had a

fleeting feeling of sympathy for Nixon, who'd at least had
the courage to admit that he did not give a damn about the
Italian lira). At twelve-thirty, just as he was preparing to go
to lunch—alone, because Claire was with Elizabeth Miller at
a UJA luncheon downtown—Justice had returned from his
errand to the press secretary's office to tell him about Briggs
and Wexford and Kineen. That had spoiled his appetite and
he hadn't bothered to eat at all.

But he had not had time to dwell on the news. At one-
fifteen there had been a brief meeting with a ceremonial
delegation from the National Council of Ministers, who were
in town for their annual convention; the bishop said he
would pray for the presidency. At one forty-five there had
been a conference with Senate Majority Leader Gordon
Parkson on S-1, a dangerous bill authored several years
before by Nixon (no sympathy this time) and John Mitchell
which would severely repress civil liberties and which was
now out of committee after nearly two years and would be
put on the Senate floor for debate. Parkson had had no
constructive ideas on how to get it back into committee or to
otherwise block it.

At two-thirty Vice-President Jim Conroy had telephoned
from Phoenix. Conroy had been making a week-long swing
through several Western states, doing a little preconvention
stumping, but had been having a fairly rough time of it: in
Montana he had had to be hurriedly taken away from his
hotel to escape an unruly crowd gathered to demonstrate in
favor of a Cheyenne Indian takeover of their reservations;
and in Wyoming he had suffered a mild case of food
poisoning at a banquet which he was convinced had not
been accidental. He said there was radical unrest in Arizona,
too, and wanted to know if he could cut the trip short and
come straight back to Washington. Augustine told him no,
repressing the urge to tell him flat out that he was not only
a whiner but a coward.

No sooner had he broken the connection than Oberdorfer

had telephoned from Tel Aviv to discuss the "Israeli crisis." Which turned out to mean that Prime Minister Stein was angry and demanding an immediate public retraction, and unless he got it was intimating that the Augustine administration would face the loss of financial and political support from the American Jewish community. Oberdorfer said ominously that careful consideration must be given to Stein's demand "or I will not be held responsible for the consequences"; Augustine said he would be in touch shortly on the matter and then hung up on him, the bastard.

Now it was after three, and he had a half-hour open before another meeting with Hendricks and Wade and Sandcrane on the damned Indian problem, and what he planned to do was to lie down on the Oval Office couch, just lie down and rest for thirty minutes. So, naturally, George Radebaugh buzzed him from the outer office and said that the attorney general wanted to see him on a matter of considerable urgency.

Christ, Augustine thought, *now* what? He picked up one of his pipes, tapped the bit wearily against his teeth. "All right," he said, "send him in."

Wexford entered immediately, and the first thing Augustine noticed about him was that he looked nervous and haggard. There was a thin coating of perspiration on his florid face that gave it a polished sheen, like a block of old carved wood. As he approached, his eyes drifted from side to side, never quite meeting Augustine's.

"Thank you for seeing me, Nicholas," he said, and sat stiffly in one of the facing chairs.

"What's the problem?"

Wexford seemed reluctant to speak. He took a handkerchief from his breast pocket and patted at his damp cheeks; he cleared his throat, seemed to find something to stare at on the terrace beyond the French doors. Intuition touched Augustine, tightened his mouth and narrowed his eyes; he was remembering what Maxwell had said to him this morning and what Justice had told him at noon. But he did not say anything, watching Julius, waiting for him to get on with it.

"Nicholas," Wexford said finally, and then stopped and cleared his throat again. "Nicholas, I've been taking soundings on this Israeli thing and I just received advance word on the new Harris poll from Austin. It looks like a twenty-two percent approval rating. Now I don't have to tell you how serious that is—"

"Get to the point, Julius," Augustine said. "You didn't come to tell me about the Harris poll."

Wexford seemed to draw himself up. "No, you're right," he said, "I didn't. I might as well be direct; the situation is painful enough without beating around the bush. The fact of the matter is, there was a rump meeting of the National Committee in Saint Louis last night, and I'm flying out there again this evening for the formal procedural discussions on the convention, and ... well, there's been a considerable amount of sentiment that it might be best for everyone—the nation, the party, even yourself—if you would decide not to seek renomination."

"I see." Carefully, Augustine laid his pipe on the desk, put his hands flat on the litter of papers before him. There was anger in him, but it was cold, controlled. He had known for weeks that something like this might happen, although he had deluded himself into believing that it would not. "And am I to believe this sentiment is based on a twenty-two percent preliminary Harris? Or is there more to it than that?"

Wexford still refused to meet his eyes. "There is no single causative factor; it's a whole pattern of feeling which has developed over recent months. And you know what's been happening in the primaries, Nicholas."

Nothing much had been happening in the primaries. Kineen had won all but one of them—the favorite-son candidate had beaten him in Pennsylvania—but he had done so over a widely split field of test-case candidates. The primaries meant little against an incumbent president anyway; even LBJ, who had lost in New Hampshire and Wisconsin in 1968, could not have been denied renomination on their basis. What primaries were, in truth, was shadow plays: clever little exercises exactly as important as the National Committee cared to make them. You could build a nomination on a series of victories, yes, as Jimmy Carter had done, as he himself had done to a lesser degree four years ago; but there were subtle ways to make sure that no victories came to a candidate the committee did not really want, and subtle ways of making even victories seem inconsequential.

Augustine said, "Either you share this sentiment, Julius, or you're the one who got the ball rolling in the first place. Which is it?"

"I share it, that's all."

"Then who did get the ball rolling? Briggs, maybe?"

"No," Wexford said, but his eyes flicked even further aside as he said it: Briggs had been a major factor, all right. "No one got the ball rolling, Nicholas. It was simply a consensus feeling on the part of the National Committee."

"Who else in the administration goes along with it?"

"Quite a few people," Wexford said. "I'm sorry, I dislike having to do this, but—"

"But you're still doing it, aren't you? Did you volunteer to be the hatchet man, or did they give you the job because no one else wanted it?"

"It was felt that because of our long-standing friendship—"

"Friendship? You're a goddamn Judas."

Wexford looked pained. "Please, Nicholas. It's not that we feel you haven't done a good job. It's just that the time has come for a change if the party is going to remain strong and unified. You must understand that."

"I understand nothing of the sort."

"It would be an unselfish and magnanimous act—"

"You're presupposing that I might be pressured into going along with the idea," Augustine said in a deceptively soft voice. "But what if I refuse? What if I decide to take my case to the people?"

A look of shock spread across Wexford's face; he was such a party politician, Augustine thought, that it was difficult for him to conceive of anyone bucking the National Committee, even the President himself. "You wouldn't do that," he said.

"Wouldn't I? I still have a few friends left."

"Yes, but not enough. My God, you'd tear the party apart."

"Not the way I see it. The party can unify around me just as easily as around Kineen; it unified around me four years ago, didn't it?"

"That was a different situation entirely," Wexford said. He was using the handkerchief again and his face had gotten as red as it had at dinner last night. "You'd better think this over carefully—don't make any hasty decisions that you'll regret later. I'll tell the committee you need time to—"

"You can tell the committee to go to hell," Augustine said. "And then you can give them my final answer: I will not make a withdrawal announcement; I am a firm candidate for reelection. Period. Now get out of here, Julius. I have nothing more to say to you."

Wexford stood up. "You're making a serious mistake, Mr. President. I urge you to reconsider."

Mr. President, Augustine thought. He did not look at Wexford. Instead he busied himself filling his pipe, tamping tobacco into the bowl from a brass humidor.

"Very well," Wexford said in flustered tones. "You have my resignation as chairman of your reelection campaign." Which was a pathetically thin exit line but one typical of the man: he turned on his heel and stalked out of the office.

Augustine got up immediately, holding the pipe between his thumb and forefinger, and opened the French doors and stepped out onto the terrace. He stood next to one of the white stone pillars, looking past the rose garden to the Jefferson Memorial in the distance.

All right, he thought, so it's come to this. A dogfight between me and Kineen. With the National Committee behind him he won't waste any time accelerating his campaign, and that means I can't waste any time with mine. Appoint a new campaign chairman right away, Ed Dougherty maybe. Make preparations for an early whistle-stopper in the Presidential Special. Challenge Kineen to a public TV appearance to debate issues. First thing, though, is to get some of the more prominent press people in here for a backgrounder; sit down with them, philosophize a bit on the presidency, answer their questions, strengthen my media image. Then—

He realized abruptly that he was putting voice to his thoughts, mumbling aloud again as he sometimes did in moments of stress. He put the pipe between his teeth, clamped down on it resolutely, and then turned back inside his office with the intention of calling Austin Briggs and having him set up the backgrounder for tomorrow morning. But just as he reached his desk the intercom buzzed—and when he flipped the toggle, George Radebaugh told him it was three forty-five and Hendricks and Wade and Sandcrane were waiting in the anteroom.

Bastards, Augustine thought, but the epithet was not meant for Hendricks and Wade and Sandcrane. I'll show them; I'll show them all. Then he said, "Have them come in," to Radebaugh, and sat down and prepared himself to talk peace treaty again with the Indians.

Ten

You look upset, Mrs. Augustine. That was Mr. Briggs on the phone, wasn't it? Did he have bad news of some kind?

I don't want to discuss it, Elizabeth.

Has something happened?

I said I don't want to discuss it.

All right, Mrs. Augustine. I'm sorry. Do you want me to leave?

No. No, don't leave. I didn't mean to be brusque. Why don't you pour us some coffee?

Here you are. May I say, Mrs. Augustine, that you were a joy to watch at the UJA luncheon today. Your remarks in defense of the President were very moving.

Thank you, Elizabeth. I've always been very competent at public affairs, haven't I.

Always.

The President relies on me to be competent.

I'm sure he does.

So does the country. They wouldn't want an emotional, incompetent First Lady, would they?

Not at all.

No, not at all. Elizabeth, what we were discussing this morning, that feeling of yours of impending tragedy. Have you discussed it with anyone else?

No, Mrs. Augustine.

Do you think anyone else feels it too?

If they do, I haven't heard anyone say it.

Good. I'm glad to hear that.

Mrs. Augustine—may I ask a question?

Certainly.

Do you have the same sort of intuition yourself?

What makes you say that?

Well, you've also been so troubled lately—

For entirely different reasons. I do not feel that there is anything terribly wrong in the White House. I'm sorry I brought up the subject again. Let's just drop it, shall we?

Yes, Mrs. Augustine.

Eleven

It was Maxwell Harper's custom, on his way home from the White House, to stop for dinner at one of Washington's better restaurants; on Wednesday evening he chose Le Consulat, in the Embassy Row Hotel. Seated in their elegant dining room, he ordered a dry martini with lemon peel and scanned the menu without finding anything that appealed to him because he was not particularly hungry. He settled finally on a Caesar salad and then sat sipping his drink and looking out at the old-Washington facades of the buildings that lined Massachusetts Avenue.

He felt bothered and fretful. The day had been filled with a series of worrisome developments, and together they added dimension to the widening pattern of administration crisis. The discussion with Augustine this morning, the President's apparent agreement with his analysis of the situation and then the abrupt termination of the meeting, as if Augustine understood what was happening around him but refused to accept the fact that it was having a pernicious effect on *him*.

The statistics released by the Department of Labor that unemployment had reached 7.4 percent nationwide. The damned S-1 bill that was now out of committee. The latest Harris poll on the Israeli gaffe. Augustine's inability to cope with the Cheyenne Indian demands for improvement of their lot, and the growing and militant support of other Amerinds, as evidenced by what had been happening to Vice-President Conroy in the West—all of which pointed toward a nasty domestic incident that would destroy the President's credibility on the human rights issue. The increasing hostility of the media. The increasing strength of Kineen and his coalition, not only in the primaries but with special-interest groups; there was a still-unconfirmed report circulating that the AFL-CIO was strongly considering support of his candidacy.

And then there was Claire Augustine.

With all those other major problems, it was probably illogical that he should be concerned about her; but the fact remained that he had not been able to get her out of his mind since their brief dialogue in the Oval Study. Was she or was she not what she had always seemed to be? Could she also be responsible in some way, directly or indirectly, for the President's weakening posture? Damn it, what went on inside that striking blonde head of hers?

The waiter arrived with a silver cart and began preparing the Caesar salad. Harper watched him distractedly, began to eat the same way when the finished salad was placed in front of him.

The problem was, he thought, Claire Augustine was a total enigma. A completely private person who seemed able to keep her public and personal lives so segregated that nothing of the real woman revealed itself. Except, perhaps, to Augustine, and of course Harper had never discussed her with the President; it was not a liberty even a personal advisor could take with the Chief Executive.

She was the daughter of a lawyer, now deceased, who had worked for the Dan O'Connell political machine in Albany, New York; she had led a somewhat sheltered childhood, having spent much of her time in private boarding schools; she had been a scholarship student at Vassar, had graduated with honors in political science and had promptly landed a secretarial post with a representative from Delaware, moving to Washington at about the same time Augustine was closing out his third term as a northern California congressman; she had been a popular figure at Washington parties, because of her beauty and her intelligence, but the rumor was that she had spurned all romantic advances, making it clear that she was a dedicated career woman.

But then she had met Augustine at one of those social gatherings—at that time he had been considered one of Washington's more eligible bachelors—and there was no way of telling if she had simply fallen in love with him or had seen in him a means to further her own ambitions. In either case, they had had one of those whirlwind courtships that culminated in marriage after four short months.

Augustine's father, Philip—a millionaire who had made his fortune as a pioneer in television electronics and who had served one term as governor of California in the mid-1940s—had died of a brain embolism during that courtship, just as Augustine was preparing to mount his campaign for reelection. Philip had been the architect of his son's political career, and it had seemed to many that Augustine might be in trouble without that strong-willed guidance. Despite her youth, however, Claire had taken an active role in the campaign, and it was generally conceded that she had made the difference between victory and defeat in a close race decided by less than ten thousand votes. Two years later she had worked tirelessly to help him win a senatorial seat—and reelection to the senate twice after that—and she had been instrumental in his successful drive for the presidency.

From all indications their marriage, too, was a happy one. When they were together publicly they interacted with ease and grace and affection, Claire remaining somewhat in the background but in such a way that her presence was always felt. The difference in their ages, as well as the difference in their emotional tendencies, appeared to be insignificant. Even the fact that they had not had any children seemed to have been by mutual consent; there had never been a hint of any incapacity in either of them.

So the upshot was that their two decades of marriage had a storybook kind of gloss: the devoted wife assisting her husband in every way to achieve his goals; the indomitable spirit and faith of the woman behind the successful man. If she had ever done anything or said anything that was in any way a negative influence on Augustine, there was no intimation of it.

And yet Harper could not quite shake the feeling that there was something different about her recently, that that difference might be working against the President. It was nothing to which he could point conclusively. An impression, that was all; a word here, a phrase there, an action or reaction that was somehow inconsistent. Still, those were things he could have misinterpreted.

He wondered if he was imagining a problem where none existed. If he was guilty of witch-hunting. It could be that: the status quo getting to him, leading him into illogical speculation—

Or was he imagining a problem because at some inner level he *wanted* one to exist between the President and the First Lady?

That thought was unsettling, but only for a moment. He was attracted to Claire Augustine, he could not deny that— and bewildered and fascinated by her. But the attraction was not that deep or that strong; it would never distort his thinking or affect his intellectual control. He was above that sort of childish emotionalism; he was incapable of it.

Harper pushed the thought away, pushed what remained of his salad away and called for the check. What he had to do, he told himself firmly, was to concentrate on facts, on finding positive measures to counteract the crisis. Action, consequence, machinery.

Before things got out of hand.

Before it was too late.

Twelve

In the Green Room, where predinner cocktails had become something of a ritual, Nicholas Augustine swallowed the last of his bourbon-and-soda and wondered if he ought to have another one. But he had had two already, and Claire was still only half-finished with her first glass of sherry, and it had only been ten minutes since they had come downstairs. Still, another drink would be pleasant; he was just beginning to feel the first two, just starting to lose some of the hard edge of tension that had built up inside him.

The glistening ice cubes in the glass drew and held his eyes. They were like precious stones, he thought; they had beauty and symmetry and elegance; and yet they were ephemeral: when you reached for them, they melted away. Like most things in life, for most people. You could look at them, covet them, even touch them, but you could never possess them. Alcohol, on the other hand, was something substantial, something attainable by everyone from peasants to kings. Alcohol—

—could lead to serious problems, he thought then, one of which was maudlin philosophizing. He wondered if he had been drinking too much lately, letting himself become too dependent on liquor. The wine at dinner last night that had gotten him through the meal but had given him the headache that still hadn't quite disappeared; the five bourbon-and-sodas at the reception for the Iranian prime minister last week that had put a faint slur on his words; the half-dozen other instances in recent weeks when he had taken one or two drinks more than necessary. If he was not careful, word would leak out to the press, and before he knew it the columnists would be comparing him to Nixon in the final days. And wouldn't Wexford and Briggs and Kineen and the rest of them love that.

Augustine smiled wryly to himself, leaned forward on his Duncan Phyfe chair to set the glass on his tray stand. As he did so he became aware that Claire was watching him from the settee opposite. She had been quiet tonight, withdrawn, as if something was weighing heavily on her mind. Her eyes, he saw, were wide and dark and fathomless. There had been a time when he felt he could perish in those eyes, that her gaze could somehow absorb him, and he had a reflection of that feeling now. But before the illusion had been sexual; now it was something else, an unknown factor.

She seemed to want to say something to him. Several seconds passed and then she sighed softly and sat forward with her hands clasped on her thighs. "Nicholas," she said, "why haven't you told me about the meeting you had with Julius Wexford this afternoon?"

Augustine stared at her. "How did you know about that?"

"Austin Briggs called me at five o'clock."

He felt an immediate surge of anger, felt heat rise on his face. He got to his feet. "Briggs," he said. "What the hell right did he have to call you?"

"He felt I should know—"

"Why? Does he want you to start working on me, too?"

"Nicholas, please."

"Answer my question. Is that why he called?"

"I suppose it was, yes."

"Well? What did you tell him?"

"I didn't tell him anything."

"But you're going to try convincing me to go along with the goddamn National Committee, aren't you."

"If I am it's not because of Austin. Or Julius, or the party, or anyone except you."

"I'm not going to withdraw," he said.

"I'm your wife, Nicholas. You've always consulted with me before, we've always made the important decisions together. Why are you excluding me this time?"

"I'm not going to withdraw," he said again. "I *can't* withdraw, I can't let them put that bastard Kineen in the White House."

"Do you really believe you can win in Saint Louis, that you can fight the National Committee *and* the special-interest groups *and* the media?"

"I overcame greater odds four years ago."

"Haven't you done enough fighting? Isn't it time to let someone else take over the battle—"

"I don't want to listen to any more of this," Augustine said. "I've had enough aggravation for one day."

"Nicholas, I'm only trying to make you understand—"

"Understand? I'm beginning to understand, all right. You're starting to turn against me too, just like the rest of them."

She flinched as if he had struck her, stood quickly and came to him and gripped his arms. He wanted to pull away from her, but her eyes held him as much as her hands. "I'm not turning against you," she said. "Don't ever say that. Don't ever think it."

He could feel the anger starting to give way; as so many times before, the nearness of her, her touch, was a kind of emotional tranquilizer. "I'm sorry, Claire, I didn't mean that. But I've taken all the pushing and shoving I can stand. My mind is made up; I need support, not dissent."

"You won't change it even for me?"

"I won't because I can't. Now I don't want to talk about it anymore."

"We have to talk about it. We ... have to."

"No," Augustine said. The anger in him was completely gone now; he felt nothing but weariness. "You asked me not to doubt you, you say you only want what's best for me—all right, then tell me you'll stand by my decision."

"Nicholas ..."

"Will you stand by *me?*" he said.

Her throat worked as if she were swallowing something painful. Her eyes moved on his face, gentle, stroking, and he knew again the illusion of being absorbed in their depths. She said, "Do you really have to ask a question like that?"

Impulsively, almost fiercely, he drew her to him, held her in a tight embrace. Felt the solid unyielding strength of her flow into him and cement his own strength. "God, how I need you," he said against the softness of her hair.

"I know," she said. "I know. I know."

Thirteen

We have gathered more evidence now against the man we believe to be the leader of the conspiracy against Nicholas Augustine—almost but not quite enough evidence to fully convict him in our eyes. We cannot afford to wait too long, and yet we must continue to be careful and cunning. The last necessary proof will come to us shortly, we are growing more and more certain of that; it can only be a matter of a day or two.

The clock ticks slowly, but it ticks inexorably too: ticks away the minutes of life that are left to this viper in the President's bosom.

Fourteen

The Oval Office, ten-thirty Thursday morning.

Christopher Justice sat in one of the chairs near the fireplace, listening as the President gave an informal interview to senior correspondents from *Time,* the Washington *Post,* and *Commentary.* The reporters—two men and a woman—were grouped in a loose semicircle before the President's desk; the only other person in the room was Austin Briggs, who occupied a chair near Justice's.

The interview had been going well. Augustine was garrulous, polite, forceful; as a result the reporters, who were clearly hostile at first, were now responding more favorably to his comments on the nature of his office, on contemporary politics, on his plans for a second term. Briggs, though, seemed nervous and kept lighting one cigarette from the butt of another. Justice wondered again why the President had asked the press secretary to sit in. For that matter, he did not know why he himself had been asked to sit in, except that Augustine seemed to want him nearby more and more of late.

The reporters' questions had gotten around now to Israel, as Justice had expected they would. The thin, attractive woman from *Time* was saying, "Mr. President, do you have anything further to add to your recent statement on Israel?"

The President smiled indulgently. "Only that those remarks of mine were meant as a comment on American foreign policy in general—a philosophical comment, not a statement of intention. In no way were they meant to demean the Israelis, as some of your colleagues have presumed."

The studious-looking man from *Commentary* leaned forward. Of the three reporters, he had been the most hostile in the beginning; Justice knew that that was because *Commentary* was an intellectual quarterly circulated almost exclusively among members of the Jewish community. "Have you conveyed that explanation to Prime Minister Stein, Mr. President?" he asked.

"Through Mr. Oberdorfer, yes, certainly."

"But reports from Tel Aviv state that the Prime Minister is demanding an immediate retraction. Apparently he was not satisfied with a simple clarification. Are we to understand, then, that you have no intention of acceding to his demand?"

"That is correct. But only because I see no purpose in retracting a misunderstood statement. It would only compound the misunderstanding, if you see what I mean—give credence to it."

"What *do* you intend to do, sir, to reestablish optimum relations with Israel?"

"Well, if Mr. Oberdorfer is unable to handle the situation to our mutual satisfaction, I will ask Prime Minister Stein to meet with me here in Washington, both privately and publicly. That should eliminate any regrettably unpleasant feelings on both sides, and help clarify our positions as friends and allies."

The man from *Commentary* seemed satisfied, as did the

other two reporters. After a moment the short, balding man from the Washington *Post* asked, "Would you care to elaborate, Mr. President, on your foreign-policy views?"

"Yes, I would," Augustine said. He selected one of his pipes, rubbed the bowl against his nose to add oil to the surface, and then buffed it vigorously with one palm. "Since the end of World War Two, our foreign policy has become the center of ideological attention; but the fact is, for many administrations it was also a means of distracting the populace from domestic problems which were not being solved. The Cold War, the arms race, escalating nuclear capabilities, the Domino Theory—all of these diverted attention from the more serious issues of racial inequality, poverty, unemployment, and so on. In short there has been a two-party consensus on foreign policy which amounts to a tacit agreement not to challenge each other on domestic affairs."

"That's an interesting concept, sir," the woman from *Time* said, "but one I find difficult to accept. Surely you don't mean that foreign policy has been overemphasized as a *deliberate* means of protecting a negative domestic status quo?"

"Not at all. I was merely pointing out that recent administrations have found domestic difficulties so insurmountable that they have concentrated instead on foreign affairs."

There were more questions, more responses on the subject, each of them increasingly complicated and philosophical. Justice had difficulty understanding some of them; political science was a topic which sometimes bewildered him.

The discussion shifted finally to Vice-President Conroy's Western states travails. Not only had he had problems in Montana and Nevada, but yesterday he had been traveling in a motorcade in Phoenix when a group of Navaho dissidents approached his open car and spat on him. A photograph showing the Vice-President cowering inside had appeared on the front pages of the Washington papers this morning, and more than one columnist had not neglected the opportunity to match Conroy's posture figuratively with that of the President. After the incident the Vice-President had gone into seclusion at his hotel and had not as yet issued a public statement.

"Mr. President," the man from the *Post* said, "what is your reaction to the incident in Phoenix?"

"I'm appalled, of course," Augustine said.

The reporter from *Commentary* asked, "Do you feel that the Vice-President was correct in not issuing a statement after the incident?"

"I see no reason why he should have. There was nothing for him to say, really."

"The photograph in this morning's papers was somewhat unflattering, to say the least. Do you question Mr. Conroy's public reaction when he was spat upon?"

"Certainly not," the President said. "I defy any man not to show fear in a similar situation."

"How do you think you might have reacted, sir, if it had been you instead of the Vice-President?"

"If you mean by that would I have retaliated in some way, the answer is yes."

"In what way, sir?"

Augustine smiled impishly. "Why, I would have unzipped my fly and pissed on the lot of them," he said.

The room became suddenly and awkwardly silent. The reporters shifted in their chairs, looking at each other, looking at the President. Briggs sat forward, the burning stub of a cigarette in one hand and an unlighted cigarette in the other; his expression was one of shock. Justice felt himself frowning, but not so much at the President's remark as at the others' reaction to it.

"After all," Augustine said lightly, "fire should be met with fire and water with water."

The silence held. When the reporter from *Commentary*

coughed into the back of his hand, the sound seemed unnaturally loud. No one moved.

The President's smile faded as he looked at the reporters. At length he tapped his pipe against an ashtray, as if calling for their attention, and then laid it aside. "That was a joke," he said. "Surely you recognize a joke when you hear one."

The man from the *Post* cleared his throat. "It's hardly a joking matter, Mr. President."

"I suppose you think it was in poor taste then."

The reporter said nothing.

"Or do you attach more significance to it than that?" the President said. His voice was low-pitched, mild, but Justice recognized an undercurrent of irascibility in the tone. "Maybe you think it was foolish, deliberately offensive?"

There was an uneasy silence this time. Justice worried his lower lip; he could feel the mood in the room shifting back to one of hostility, knew that the President must feel it too. And yet Augustine seemed to be offended by their attitude—with cause, Justice thought, because the joke had not been all that improper—and unwilling to let the issue pass. As a result of that, if not of the joke itself, all the goodwill he had established in the past hour seemed threatened.

"No comment, eh?" the President said. "Well then, maybe the press secretary has something to say. How about it, Austin? What's your opinion of my little joke?"

Briggs was startled. "Mr. President?"

"You heard me, Austin. What's your opinion?"

The three reporters had turned to look at Briggs. He glanced at them nervously, said, "I have no opinion, sir."

"No? Do you think we ought to make it an off-the-record comment?"

"Well ... that might be best, yes—"

"I agree," Augustine said. "We wouldn't want these distinguished writers to pass it along to their readers and risk a misinterpretation of its meaning and intent. Not that they would misinterpret it themselves, of course."

Briggs looked down at his burning cigarette, stubbed it out in the ashtray beside him without speaking.

The President nodded and sat back in his chair. "Now that that's settled," he said to the reporters, "shall we go on to another topic?"

They had been exchanging looks again, and Justice could tell from their profiles that Augustine had lost them. The woman from *Time* said stiffly, "I don't believe we have any more questions at this time, Mr. President."

"I see." Augustine's voice had turned cool, distant. "All right, then we'll consider the interview terminated. Thank you for your attendance. Mr. Briggs will show you out."

When the reporters were gone, and Briggs was gone, the President picked up the toy locomotive and sat studying it as if looking for flaws in its construction. Justice watched him for a time and then got to his feet and crossed to stand in front of the desk.

"Mr. President?" he said. "Do you want me to leave too?"

Augustine did not look up. "Yes, Christopher, I'd rather you did."

"Yes sir," Justice said, and wanted to say something else, something comforting. But what words could someone like him offer that would have any meaning?

He turned reluctantly and left the President alone.

Fifteen

Maxwell Harper had been looking for the President for thirty minutes before he finally found him: strolling through the rose garden with his bodyguard, Justice, and humming one of those damned railroad folk songs.

Augustine stopped humming when Harper came up to them, squinted his eyes against the glare of the late-afternoon sun. It had been one of those sultry Washington false-summer days, temperature in the eighties, seventy percent humidity, and Augustine had loosened his tie and shed his suit jacket. His shirt was heat-rumpled and damp with patches of perspiration. There was a thin gleam of sweat on his forehead as well. His eyes and his mouth were solemn.

Harper said, "We have to talk, Mr. President."

"All right, Maxwell. Go ahead."

"In private."

"We can talk in front of Christopher," Augustine said. "He's on our side, you know."

"I think it would be best if we spoke alone."

Justice moved his feet in a self-conscious way. Unlike the President, he still wore his jacket and his tie was crisply knotted. He said to Augustine, "I can wait for you inside, sir . . ."

"Nonsense. I prefer to have you here."

Harper felt his hands clenching, an old habit when he was upset and one he hated in himself. But how could he be expected to maintain rigid control in the face of a crisis that, in spite of him, grew graver by the day? He wanted to say that this was hardly a matter to be discussed in front of a Secret Service bodyguard, of all people, but he curbed the impulse. There was no sense in arguing the point.

"Very well," he said. "I suppose you know about the UPI story that broke a little while ago."

"Yes," Augustine said, "I know about it. I had a call from Senator Jackman just before I came out here."

"How accurate was their quote?"

"Fairly accurate. They paraphrased, of course."

"Then you really did say you would have urinated on those dissidents in Phoenix?"

"No, I said I would have pissed on them."

"What?"

"Don't look so shocked, Maxwell," Augustine said. "I realize the word *piss* is still considered a little vulgar at Harvard and the Institute of Policy Studies, but it really isn't, you know. It's just a word. Besides, I was making a joke."

"Joke?"

"Exactly. Isn't that so, Christopher?"

"Yes sir," Justice said.

Augustine nodded. "A harmless little joke."

Harper stared at him. For an instant he felt as though he were standing there with a pair of ciphers instead of just one; that all of the President's intellect had been abrogated, reducing him to a witless figurehead who prattled on about semantics and making jokes.

Trying to keep his tone reasonable, he said, "Mr. President, didn't you realize the repercussions of a statement like that?"

"Belatedly," Augustine said, but there was no apology in his tone. "Which is why I specifically stated that the comment was to be taken off the record."

"Off the record? Then how did it leak out to UPI? Unless it was the *Post* reporter ..."

"It wasn't the *Post* reporter. I've known him for years and he can be a bastard at times, but he would never betray a direct Presidential request. Neither would the other two."

"Then who was responsible?"

"There was only one other person present besides Christopher," the President said. "I shouldn't have asked him to sit in, I was a damned fool for doing it, but I thought it would be a psychological advantage to have him there, let him see how I was going to handle the media."

"For God's sake—Briggs?"

Augustine nodded. The sun burning against his face illuminated it so brightly that the lines on his cheeks and around his eyes appeared deep and sharply etched, like the scars of old wounds. "Briggs," he said. "I didn't expect he'd go this far, but I should have known he was capable of it."

Harper's hands had clenched again; he flattened them out against his hips. "I suppose we've all been guilty of underestimating people."

"Yes. Well, Briggs is a dangerous man, there's no question of that now. Something has to be done about him."

"Granted. But what?"

"That's what I've been trying to decide, walking out here with Christopher."

"And?"

"And—I don't know; I just don't know. I could fire him, that's the obvious choice—"

"It's also the worst thing you could do right now," Harper said. "It would make a martyr out of him."

"I know that, Maxwell. I've already discarded the idea."

The collar of Harper's shirt felt tight, sticky, but he did not lift a hand to loosen his tie. If Justice could stand the heat properly dressed, so could he. He felt Justice looking at him then, glanced at the man and saw his own frustration mirrored in the steady brown eyes; he put his gaze back on Augustine.

The President said, "There's got to be another way."

"I don't envision it yet if there is. Beyond your being very careful, that is, not to make any more controversial remarks—no candid comments, no jokes, nothing that can be misinterpreted or deliberately taken out of context."

"I have every intention of being careful," Augustine said. "From now on I'll exclude Briggs from press conferences and other public appearances; I've already informed him by memo that he is not to join us on the trip to The Hollows this weekend. But that won't stop him. No, there *has* to be some sort of direct action. And someone has to find it damned soon."

Harper was silent. The three of them stood in the hot sun, listening to the faint hum of a lawn mower somewhere on the grounds, the murmur of traffic and voices from the East Gate as the last of the White House tour groups left for the day. Listening to their own thoughts.

Augustine said finally, "Isn't that so, Maxwell?"

"Yes," Harper said. "Someone will have to find a way."

Sixteen

We have all the evidence now that we need: the traitor stands convicted. And the hour of his execution is at hand.

When we slip quietly into the press secretary's office, the anteroom is dark and as deserted as the West Wing corridors; it is after nine o'clock and nearly all the White House staff has left for the day. But there is a strip of light showing beneath the door of the traitor's private office. He is waiting for us just as we requested by telephone at five o'clock. Even though we did not tell him why we wanted to see him at such a late hour, he agreed to the meeting without question. In that sense only he is an ideal press secretary—a man whose time is perceived solely in terms of how others will utilize it.

We open the door without knocking, step inside. Briggs has been sitting on the leather couch against one wall and he frowns when we come in, probably in reaction to our unannounced entrance. Then he stands, puts aside a sheaf of press clippings he has been reading and comes forward. He does not smile as he faces us.

He seems to want to say something about observing the proprieties before entering one's private domain, but he is too used to a role of passive servility to assert himself to anyone who represents authority. Instead he says, "Well, right on time."

"Yes," we say, "right on time."

"Well—would you care to sit down?"

"We'd ... *I'd* rather stand." Careful. Careful.

"All right." He takes a package of cigarettes from his shirt pocket, extracts one, lights it with a silver lighter, and blows smoke carefully to one side. "Well," he says for the third time, "what is it you wanted to see me about? I had the impression on the phone that it was important."

"It is," we say, and move past him, stop beside his desk and pretend to look through the open venetian blinds at the lighted grounds beyond. We let the fingers of our left hand slide along the desk, come to rest on the smooth black onyx ashtray we have seen there before. Then we turn slowly to face Briggs again.

His head is wreathed in smoke from his cigarette. A thin streamer of it rises from his hand in a vertical line that seems to bisect his face, so that for an instant we see him as two fragmented halves, as if he has been cleaved in two. The image is unsettling and we take a step backward and one more to our left—but not so far away from the desk that we cannot now reach the black onyx ashtray with our right hand.

Briggs says, "If it has something to do with the backgrounder this morning—"

"It has everything to do with that," we say, "and nothing to do with it. I'm here because of you—what you are and what you've tried to do."

He avoids our eyes, puffs deeply on his cigarette. "I don't know what you mean," he says.

"Oh but you do. You know exactly what I mean."

His expression becomes defensive. "My conscience is clear," he says. "I've never done anything that wasn't in the best interests of the party, the presidency, the country."

"Not to mention the best interests of Austin Briggs."

"That's not true."

"Isn't it?" We look at him more closely, and what we see feeds our hatred for him, cements our purpose. "You're a parasite, Austin, and a righteous, self-deluding one at that. You don't have an ounce of compassion or human decency."

He stiffens, looks at us, looks away. There is a stirring of fear in him now; we can see it in his eyes. "I don't have to listen to that," he says.

"No, of course you don't. There's no point in going on with it, is there?"

"None at all," Briggs says, and draws again on his cigarette.

"You're about to lose your ash," we say.

He blinks. "What?"

"The ash on your cigarette, you're about to lose it," we say. And we pick up the black onyx ashtray, cup it in our palm, extend it toward him.

"Oh," he says in a confused way, "yes." He takes a step forward, and his gaze is locked on the ashtray; he does not notice that we have braced one hip against the desk, that we stand rigid and poised. Our heart is racing wildly now.

When he reaches out with his cigarette for the ashtray we raise our left hand and jab the knuckles sharply into his shoulder. He stops in mid-stride, frowning in surprise, and turns his head toward his shoulder—and that exposes his left temple, makes of it a target on which we fasten our own gaze. Then we bring the ashtray up with all our strength and drive the flat edge of it against his temple.

There is a dull, ugly sound. Briggs cries out in pain,

staggers but does not fall. We go after him, swing the ashtray a second time, feel it connect solidly with the bone above one eye. This time he makes no sound and this time he collapses immediately, boneless, and lies staring up at us with eyes like discs of polished glass.

The execution is finished: the traitor is dead.

We take several deep breaths, look away from Briggs and cock our head to listen. No one has heard his cry; the building is shrouded in silence. We realize his dropped cigarette is smoldering on the carpet, and we pick it up and tamp it out in the ashtray which we find we are still holding in our hand. On the carpet is a small black scorch mark, but there is nothing to be done about that. The ashtray is undamaged, and since the blows we struck did not draw blood, there are no marks on it. We replace it on the desk.

It occurs to us as we go to the window that we have, in spite of all our premeditation, acted with too much passion and not enough foresight in our planning. We might have chosen a better place for Briggs's execution than his own office, than the White House. But it is too late to worry about that now. What is done is done.

We roll up the blinds, bind them into place, then unlatch the window and open it. Carefully we put our head out into the muggy night air. Floodlights illuminate the rose garden, the trees and shubbery on the south lawn, but the oleander bushes beneath the window are wrapped in shadow. Over by the south balcony, we see one of the security people walking his patrol—but after a moment he disappears around the east corner. There is no one else within the range of our vision; night security on the grounds is considerable, but it is also concentrated at the perimeters to guard against illegal entry.

We open the window all the way, return quickly to where Briggs lies sprawled on the carpet. We grasp him under the armpits, struggle with his inert weight to the window, and manage to lift him across the sill. Perspiration spots our forehead; the effort of moving Briggs has left us panting. We take a moment to catch our breath, looking out again at the grounds. They still appear deserted in all directions.

Leaning our shoulder against Briggs's hip, we push him over the sill.

He falls loosely, making a whispery rustling sound in the oleanders and then a barely audible thump as he strikes the ground—not heavy enough to register on the sound-sensor equipment monitored by Security. When we peer down we see him lying in a pocket of heavy shadow, his arms folded under him, his head resting near one of several large decorative stones which border the oleanders. Our plan will work after all, we think. It will appear as though he was leaning out of the window, lost his balance, fell and struck his head on one of those stones. A tragic accident.

We turn from the window, leaving it open, and glance around the office. There is nothing out of place, no signs of violence. Satisfied, we cross to the door, open it, slip into the anteroom; and a moment later our steps echo hollowly in the empty corridor as we hurry away from the scene of our execution.

The scene of our act of mercy.

Seventeen

It was 10:25 when the telephone rang in the Oval Study.

The sudden sound made Augustine jerk his head up from *Fred Fearnot and the Rioters,* the Hal Standish railroad dime novel he was paging through. He looked at the Seth Thomas wall clock, noted the time. Pretty late for someone to be calling, he thought, unless it's important business. He let the phone ring three more times while he rubbed at his tired eyes, took a sip of water from the tumbler on his desk blotter. Then he reached out and caught up the receiver.

"Yes?"

"Mr. President? This is Christopher Justice, sir. I have to see you right away. It's urgent."

"Urgent? At this time of night?"

"Yes sir, very urgent."

"Where are you?"

"Downstairs in the press secretary's office."

"All right—come up then."

"Thank you, sir."

Augustine replaced the receiver. Justice's voice had

sounded grim, shaken, as if he were the harbinger of tragic news; and it would have to *be* something tragic, Augustine thought, to rattle someone of Christopher's nature. A foreboding touched him, but it was ephemeral, directionless. He could not imagine what might have happened.

He picked up the dime novel again, carried it around his desk and across the room, and put it away in one of the glass-fronted cabinets. Restlessly he began to roam the study. Two minutes passed; three. He had stopped in front of the shelves of railroad lanterns and was running his fingers over the flared reflectors on one of them when the knock, soft but hurried, sounded on the door.

When he opened the door, the sense of foreboding deepened. Justice's face was tightly set; his eyes, shadowed because of the dim light in both the hallway and the study, had a somber, uneasy appearance.

Augustine gestured him inside, shut the door. "My God, Christopher," he said, "what is it, what's happened?"

Justice said heavily, "It's Mr. Briggs, sir."

"Briggs?"

"Yes sir. He ... I'm afraid he's dead."

"What!"

"It's true, Mr. President. I was walking on the south lawn, getting some air because it was so hot in my room, and I noticed that the window in the press secretary's office was open and the lights were on. But there was nobody inside, so I went over to have a look. I found him lying in the bushes under the window."

"But *how*—how did it happen?"

"I'm not sure, sir. It looks as though he was leaning out for some reason and lost his balance and fell. He must have hit his head on one of the rocks."

A hollowness had formed under Augustine's breastbone, but he seemed to have no other reaction beyond a kind of shocked confusion. Sometimes you came up against something so stunning that you lacked the emotional language to deal with it immediately. He shook his head, walked over to the nearest piece of furniture—a leather couch—and sat on the arm and stared down at the carpet.

Across the study, the door to the presidential bedroom opened and Claire entered. "I thought I heard voices," she said. "Is something—" Then she stopped speaking and ridges appeared on the smooth surface of her forehead.

Augustine said, "Claire, something terrible has happened."

A shadow passed across her face. She caught the fabric of her blouse at the throat—she was still fully dressed, or she would not have entered as she had—and then came over to where he was sitting. "What is it?"

"It's Austin Briggs. He's dead."

Her mouth opened and her face went white. "Oh my God," she said.

"Christopher just found him, outside his office window."

"Where?"

"It seems to have been a freak accident, Mrs. Augustine," Justice said. He went on to tell her what he had told Augustine.

Claire said, "Are you certain he's dead?"

"Yes ma'am. I checked his pulse."

"Have you told anyone else?"

"No. I thought the President should be the first to know."

She closed her eyes, put her hands to her temples as though trying to clear her thoughts. Watching her, Augustine thought dully that the news seemed to have hit her even harder than it had him; he had never seen her quite so shaken.

Justice said, "Do you want me to notify the security chief, Mr. President?"

Before Augustine could answer, Claire lowered her hands and turned abruptly. "No," she said. "Not yet. Don't call anyone yet."

"But Mrs. Augustine . . ."

"Don't argue with me, please. We need time to think."

Justice looked at Augustine, who nodded mutely. "Yes ma'am," he said then. "Whatever you say."

Claire bit her lip, and her eyes, dark and glistening, rested on Augustine for a long moment. Then she pivoted and hurried out of the study.

When the bedroom door closed behind her Augustine roused himself, went slowly to his desk and poured water into the tumbler there; drank it to ease the dryness in his throat. Some of the numbness began to leave him then, and in his mind he heard the echo of Claire's voice saying *We need time to think.* Time to think about what? Briggs was dead, he had died in a tragic accident. In one sense it was unfortunate; and yet, looking at it another way, coldly and practically, it solved the problem of his political threat.

Time to think about what?

But it was already beginning to break in on Augustine, the same realization that must have struck Claire immediately: it was not the fact of Briggs's death that demanded careful reflection, but the probable repercussions of it. He had died here at the White House, and under circumstances which were as bizarre as they were tragic. There had probably never been an accidental death on the White House grounds, no deaths of any kind here that he was aware of since President Harrison had succumbed to pneumonia in 1841. The story would make national headlines, would have the country buzzing for weeks. Members of the press and his political enemies would use it as a weapon to further attack the viability of the Augustine administration; some of the more vicious, muckraking types might even hint at Christ knew what type of scandal.

Augustine passed a hand roughly over his face. Time to think, time to think—but what was there to be done? Briggs was already dead. Still, the real problem was not the death itself, it was where and how he had died. If the accident had happened somewhere else, in his own house in Cleveland Park, for instance, the repercussions might not be so—

Somewhere else, he thought.

Justice had not told anyone about finding Briggs; suppose it were possible to move the body, to take it away from the White House, to put it in another place where an accidental fall might have happened, a place such as Briggs's home? *Could* a dead man be transported off the grounds with all the security guards and security devices in operation? Maybe, he thought. If the man who moved the body was a Secret Serviceman himself, whose presence on the grounds at night would arouse no suspicion, would not be questioned; if the man was Christopher Justice—

No, he thought then, angry with himself, it's a criminal offense, for God's sake, I won't be a party to a thing like that. All his life he had prided himself on his honesty, on his steadfast code of decency in government. If he compromised his principles now, how could he live with his conscience?

And what if Justice were caught? He would have to be sworn to absolute silence in any event, which meant that if he *were* caught, he would be forced to accept full and sole responsibility—and that would lead to public disgrace, an end to his career, and to repercussions that would be just as bad as if Briggs's death were simply reported as it ought to be. Ordering him to take that kind of risk was a terrible inequity.

And yet . . .

If Justice were careful, he would not be caught; he was a resourceful man, a cautious man; the odds were good that he *could* get away with it. Wasn't it worth the risk, then, in the long run? After all, a cover-up of this sort wasn't really so awful; he would only be taking steps to counteract a bitter turn of fate, to save the country from disruptive hue and cry, to save himself and his administration from the kind of attacks that could cost him renomination and reelection. Didn't all of that vindicate a minor transgression, a minor distortion of the truth? And where Justice was concerned, wasn't it a simple if painful matter of priority? The sacrifice of one common man meant little enough compared to the welfare of the country and of the President; Justice would understand that without having to be told, and because he was both loyal and trusting, he would accept the order without question.

Augustine stood for a while longer, struggling with himself; but at a deeper level he had already made his decision, right or wrong. Still, even when he admitted it to himself finally, he knew he would have to talk to Claire. This was one decision he could not act on without discussing it with her first.

He pushed away from the desk, saw Justice standing uneasily by the hall door. "I'll be back in a minute," he said. "Wait here, Christopher. Don't do anything until I come back."

"Yes sir."

Claire was in her bedroom, and when Augustine entered he was surprised to find her just hanging up the telephone extension there. She seemed more composed now; the stricken look was gone and some of the rocklike stability that was the cornerstone of her personality had returned. It was always that way with her: no matter what crisis might arise, she never allowed it to disturb her poise for long.

He said, "Whom were you talking to?"

"The appointments secretary," she said. Her voice was thick. "I've asked him to make arrangements for us to leave for The Hollows first thing tomorrow morning."

"The Hollows?"

"It's best if we don't stay in Washington at a time like this."

"Yes, you're probably right," Augustine said slowly. "The only thing is, how will it look if we leave so soon after the announcement of Briggs's death?"

She came forward, stopped so close to him that he could feel the warmth of her breath on his face. "There doesn't have to be an announcement tonight, does there?" she said. "There doesn't have to be an announcement for a while yet."

Those wide hypnotic eyes gripped his own, probed into them with such intensity that it was as if she were able to penetrate his mind and read his thoughts, to touch the soul of him. She knew him so well, so well; no part of him could ever remain secret to her for very long. Relief moved through him: the decision was theirs, not his, and it was bound.

"No," he said, "not if the body were to be moved to Briggs's house in Cleveland Park, if it appeared that that was where he had his accident."

"Do you think that can be done?"

"Yes. It's a dangerous risk, but I think it can. And I think we have to try it, Claire. I hate the deception of it, and yet we can't afford not to handle it this way."

"I know," she said. "But you won't do it yourself?"

"Of course not. Christopher will have to do it."

"Alone, Nicholas. Promise me you'll stay here with me."

Augustine nodded, hating himself just a little in that moment. "I'd better tell him," he said. "We don't have much time; the body could be discovered at any second."

"Yes," she said. "At any second."

He turned, went to the door. As he opened it he glanced back and saw that she had sat down on the rosewood bed; her head was bowed, and he thought he saw the gleam of wetness on one cheek. Tears? But she never cried; he had never seen her cry once in twenty years of marriage.

He swallowed against a sudden constriction in his throat, walked into his bedroom and through it to the study to face Justice. *Forgive me,* he thought—and did not know if he was asking forgiveness of Claire or Justice or God or the world.

Eighteen

There was no one in the immediate area when Justice pulled his Ford Sedan under the portico on the West Wing's north side, parked it there in the shadows. Far down near the carriage entrance to the White House proper, a pair of civil-service guards stood looking across at Lafayette Park; he had stopped the car to talk to them briefly, as he had done with two other sets of guards on his way here from the staff parking lot, telling each of them that the President had asked him to deliver a box of file papers from one of the West Wing offices to Senator Jackman's home in Georgetown. No one had questioned him; there was no reason they should have. And since his car was known to the rest of the security staff, none of the other guards would think anything about it if they came across the Ford parked here under the portico.

Justice got out of the car, stepped around to the rear and unlocked the trunk but did not raise the lid. Then he walked back to the West Wing corner, went around it toward the south wall. When he reached it he stopped to listen, to scan the south grounds. Everything appeared quiet, normal. A thin, hot breeze rustled the shrubbery nearby, otherwise the night was hushed, scented with cloying spring fragrances. Reflected light shimmered on the surfaces of one of the ponds; there was a faint whitish glow on the horizon cast by the lights in the Jefferson Memorial. There was no sign of any of the guards in the vicinity.

He hurried out onto the lawn, staying in close to the building where there were long patches of shadow. Except for the lighted rectangle that marked the press secretary's office, halfway between the west corner and the Oval Office portico, all of the ground-floor windows were dark. Yellowish illumination showed at two of the second floor windows, but unless someone up there was standing close to the panes and looking straight down, he would not be seen.

Justice's face felt damp and hot, and he ducked it against the sleeve of his suit jacket as he went. Ever since leaving the Oval Study twenty minutes ago, he had kept his mind deliberately blank; he had learned in the military, and again in the Secret Service's indoctrination courses, that when you were given a mission of any kind—and particularly one which involved peril—the only way to perform it properly was to close your mind to everything but the mission itself.

But like an undercurrent, thoughts and emotions kept tugging at him. Bewilderment: too many things happening too quickly, in a way and with implications that he lacked the capacity to understand. Furtiveness, wrongness: he was an officer of the law, he had dedicated his life to upholding it, and yet here he was, about to commit an act which was contrary to the very codes by which he lived. A sense of fatalism: he was not going to get away with this, there were too many things that could go wrong, too many obstacles to overcome. Faith in the President: if he had been surprised and disconcerted by the order to move Briggs's body, he had also immediately understood and accepted Augustine's explanation of why it was necessary. He knew well enough what would happen to him if he *were* discovered, but that did not bother him; the greater good was all that mattered. All that mattered.

When he neared the lighted window he stopped and drew a heavy, silent breath. Standing just outside the elongation of light, he looked back toward the west corner. Stillness. He moved his gaze across the lawn, past the dark squares of the helicopter landing pad, around toward the rose garden. Satisfied that he was alone, he bent at the waist and went quickly to the oleander bushes beneath the window, spread them cautiously with his hands until he had access to the press secretary's body.

He pulled at the one outflung arm and it yielded limply; Briggs had not been dead long enough for rigor mortis to set in. Justice got a firm grip on the arm, another grip on the trousers at the hip, and dragged the body out of the bushes and across the bordering stones. The small rustling scraping sounds he made seemed unnaturally loud in his ears. He paused, down on one knee, and looked up at the illuminated second-story windows. They remained empty.

Justice rubbed sweat from his eyes, got a two-handed purchase on Briggs's arm and hoisted the body up across his back in a fireman's carry. The skin on his neck crawled where Briggs's hair brushed it; he shifted the weight slightly until the head lay canted against his shoulder. Then he shoved up, and once he had his balance, once he was sure the body wasn't going to slip, he began to run humped-over back to the west corner.

The muggy night air burned in his lungs and he could hear himself breathing in thin, ragged pants, but he did not break stride until he neared the corner. Ten feet from it he veered over to the wall and braced his free shoulder against it, got his breathing under control. He listened. All around him the night held its spring hush.

He put his head around the corner—and one of the civil-service guards was walking at an angle parallel with the far wall, toward where the Ford was parked under the portico.

Justice pulled his head back, stood tensed. Had the guard seen him? But he hadn't been looking in this direction, had been moving at an easy pace with eyes toward the Ford. He let twenty seconds pass, heard nothing, and eased his head around the corner again.

No sign of the guard.

He stepped off the lawn, striding more rapidly than before because of the absence of shadow here, and when he neared the north corner the muscles in his legs and back were knotted from the weight of the body, the strain of running with it. Nothing to be done about that. He could not put it down, not here; it would take too much time, too much effort to lift it again, and he did not know where the guard he had seen walking was now.

The lights of a car drifted by the old Executive Office Building on Seventeenth Street, briefly touched the guard booths far down at the West Gate. There was no movement from that direction: he had not been spotted from there. Justice craned forward to peer out along the north wall, saw the one guard moving away past the carriage entrance. The other two guards who had been standing there were gone.

Setting his teeth, he made the run to the north portico and the rear of his car.

Three-quarters of the way there he felt his legs begin to give out. Panic gripped him; he had an image of himself sprawled out on the blacktop with the body beside him, people shouting and converging on him. He forced himself to slow to a staggering walk, saw the car loom larger ahead of him and automatically extended his left hand, reaching for it. His fingers touched the warm metal of the trunk, fumbled for the bottom edge and found it and lifted the lid just as a cramp buckled his left leg. He felt himself falling, twisted against the rear bumper—and Briggs's body rolled off his back and inside the trunk.

Justice heard it hit something metallic, sending small,

ringing echoes into the night, as he jarred painfully onto his right knee. The sweat on his body turned cold; he caught the bumper, used it to push himself half-erect. He dragged the trunk lid down, had to curb an impulse to slam it and pressed down on it instead until the lock clicked. Then he leaned against it and jerked his head around in desperate quadrants because he was sure he had just made enough noise to alert anyone within a hundred-yard radius.

He saw no one. Even the lone guard had vanished into the night shadows.

In the new silence he pushed away from the trunk, stood unsteadily for a moment. Pain throbbed in his knee; there was a prickly sensation of weakness in both thighs, both calves. He got his handkerchief out and mopped at the film of moisture on his face as he limped around to the driver's door, opened it and moved inside. His hands trembled slightly on the wheel, but by the time he had gotten the car started and pointed toward the West Gate, they were steady again.

No one came running out of the White House; no one challenged him at all.

By the time he reached the gate his pulse rate had decelerated to normal. He had no trouble with the guards there; they knew him and passed him through with a brief exchange of amenities and only cursory attention to procedure.

The raw edge of tension left him as he drove slowly to Pennsylvania Avenue, turned northwest. He had done it; amazingly, in spite of the odds and his feeling of fatalism, he had gotten clear of the White House grounds with Briggs's body and without incident. But the mission was not over yet. Something could still go wrong if he was not careful.

The President had told him that Briggs lived in a private house on Arden Place in Cleveland Park, out in the old county—a thirty-minute drive even at this time of night. Justice glanced at his watch: nearly midnight. Good. The later it was, the less likely the chance of anyone noticing him while he completed the transfer.

Traffic was light on Pennsylvania Avenue, and as he drove along it he found himself thinking strangely of the funeral procession carrying the body of President Kennedy to Arlington National Cemetery. Or maybe not so strangely at all. Weren't he and his car, traveling part of the same route, also a kind of miniature funeral procession transporting the body of the press secretary?

A chill caressed his neck. He imagined that he could hear caissons, the thunder of drums, the clattering hooves of horses—echoes in his memory of that long-ago day in 1963. He had been nineteen at the time, attached to a military police unit stationed at Fort Benning; young and somewhat callous, not quite as stricken by the assassination as most of the country, as most of the other army personnel. He had spent a good part of those four days after the shooting drinking beer at the PX; routine had been completely disrupted, and for him and most of his company that had been an excuse for taking an extended pass. At the exact moment the casket had been taken out onto Pennsylvania Avenue—he remembered this distinctly—he had been standing half-drunk at the PX bar, watching television and arguing with two other MPs over whether the National Football League commissioner had the right idea in going ahead with the schedule on Sunday or whether it showed a lack of respect.

It was not that he himself had been disrespectful. No, it was only that he had never been an emotional man. Until now, these past few weeks. For the first time he could feel the full weight of the assassination, of what the loss of the President had done to the country—and he knew it was because the crisis facing Nicholas Augustine, *his* President, threatened a similar if not quite so tragic loss.

He turned the Ford north on Twenty-third Street, then northwest again on Massachusetts Avenue. When he reached Cleveland Park—a quiet residential area that had once been the summer retreat of President Grover Cleveland—he pulled to the curb and consulted the map of Washington he kept in the glove compartment. Fifteen minutes later he brought the Ford onto Arden Place, a short dead-end street shaded by Dutch elms and sycamores.

The houses on both sides were all turn-of-the-century dwellings with cupolas and wide front porches, set well back from the street and spaced widely apart. Briggs's address was in the last block, and the first thing Justice noticed about it was that the driveway was bordered by cherry trees on one side and shrubbery on the other. He drove past, looking at the neighboring houses on each side and across the street. The only ones which showed light were on the opposite side and some distance removed.

He made a U-turn where Arden Place ended at the edge of a park, came back and turned into Briggs's drive. His headlights picked up a small side porch heavily grown with ivy, the closed doors of a garage that would be empty because Briggs did not drive. Which was good because it eliminated the problem of having to move a car.

Once he had drawn abreast of the porch Justice braked to a stop and shut off the lights. Darkness surrounded him when he stepped out; there was a street lamp diagonally across the way, but its glow did not reach into the driveway. He opened the trunk, reached in to turn the body so that he could get at the pockets in its clothing. It was just starting to stiffen, but not so much yet that it presented a problem. In the right trouser pocket he found a key case, drew it out and then closed the trunk again and hurried up onto the porch.

The third key he tried opened the door there. He slipped inside, stood for a moment to let his eyes adjust. The kitchen: enough moonlight penetrated through a window in the rear wall to let him see the shapes of refrigerator and stove and sink cabinet. Should he leave the body here? Plenty of home accidents happened in the kitchen, and if he put Briggs here he would not have to turn on any lights—

No. The body had lain on the ground beneath the window, it was lying now on the trunk floor; Briggs's suit would be dirty, maybe even torn in places. The bathroom then, that was the only safe place to put him. Bathroom accidents were even more common than kitchen ones.

Justice made his way carefully to a doorway in the inner wall, found himself in a central corridor. He brushed his fingers along the wall there and located a light switch—he had to risk putting on the lights—and flipped the toggle. A ceiling globe came on, filling the corridor with a pale yellow glow. Blinking, he turned to his left and tried three doors before discovering the bathroom. Immediately, then, he returned to the kitchen and went outside again into the muggy darkness.

It took him twenty minutes to get the body out of the trunk and into the bathroom, to strip it of jacket, trousers, shirt, tie, and shoes, leaving it clad only in socks and soiled underwear, and to position it on the floor with the head between the toilet and the old-fashioned cast-iron bathtub. He examined the clothing. The jacket was ripped in two places and there were grass stains and a smear of grease on the pants; he wadded both articles together, put them on the sink. The shirt and the socks went into a clothes hamper, and he took the tie and the shoes into the bedroom, put the shoes beside the bed and hung the tie on a rack in one of the closets.

He was sweating again when he finished; his mouth tasted dry, brassy. He went back into the bathroom, looked down at the body. Had he overlooked anything? In the mystery novels he read and collected there was always something overlooked, something forgotten, that the clever detective would notice—

Mystery novels. Clever detectives.

He shook himself, tried to concentrate on the scene in front of him. Briggs's hair, he thought. It was badly mussed and it would not have been that way if he had simply come in here, slipped and fallen against the bathtub.

Justice lifted a hairbrush from the counter beside the sink, knelt next to the body and managed to sweep the hair back into place. Straightening, he replaced the brush. Anything else? No. Everything appeared natural now, nothing out of place.

He caught up the suit jacket and trousers, reentered the bedroom, and laid Briggs's key case on the dresser next to the wallet and the other articles he had removed from the suit. Then, leaving the lights on in the bathroom, the bedroom, and the center hall, he went through the kitchen and set the push-button lock on the porch door. Outside, the night was still empty, quiet. He closed the door softly behind him, hurried into the Ford.

The street was deserted in both directions when he backed out of the drive. The only house lights in the block were three hundred yards distant; he swung the car in the opposite direction.

And it was done.

Justice tried to make himself relax now. But he was still keyed up; he imagined a dozen things that could go wrong, a dozen mistakes he might have made. He kept reviewing the past three hours, but instead of remaining clear and vivid in his memory, they took on a kind of surreal, extrinsic quality, as if he had watched it all happen—or read it all happen—instead of having done it himself.

And as he guided the Ford through the empty streets of Cleveland Park, there was fear in him. It was abrupt and insidious, different from the fear of discovery or the fear of error, different from any fear he had ever known.

Because it had no name.

PART TWO
The Presidential Special

One

Painted a gleaming red, white and blue, its big diesel locomotive rumbling steadily in the warm Los Angeles afternoon, the Presidential Special reminded Augustine, not for the first time, of a sleek faithful animal awaiting the arrival of its master. As he crossed the Union Station platform surrounded by aides and Secret Servicemen, Claire with her arm tucked around his, he gazed fondly at the ten cars in the string: baggage car, train staff's car, security personnel's Pullman, specially outfitted communications car, the old SP parlor car which he had had converted into an office and conference room and private compartments for himself and Claire and which he had dubbed U.S. Car Number One, aides' Pullman, dining car, club car, and finally the glass-roofed observation car with its open rear platform. And he felt the familiar stir of excitement that always came to him when he was about to embark on this train, *his* train.

His spirits had been at a low ebb since last night; even Justice's report that the transference of Briggs's body had been accomplished without incident had failed to ease his mind. But now that he was in California again, approaching the Presidential Special and soon to be at The Hollows, a sense of optimism had begun to return to him. He always seemed to feel more sanguine about things when he was away from the Washington milieu, the austere atmosphere of the White House. Truman had been right: no man in his right mind would ever enjoy living in that place. And that, of course, was why all the presidents in the past several decades had taken every opportunity to go elsewhere—Roosevelt to Warm Springs, Truman himself to Independence, Eisenhower to Camp David, Kennedy to the family home in Hyannisport, Johnson to his Texas ranch, Nixon to Key Biscayne and San Clemente and Camp David, Carter to his Georgia farm. Despite all the negativism in the press about his own California trips, Augustine thought, the simple truth was that a "Washington Presidency" was a figment of the Constitution. The country could be run just as effectively outside the Capital.

He smiled at Claire as they neared U.S. Car Number One, to let her know he felt cheered, but her answering smile was preoccupied and mechanical. Her mood had matched his in the past eighteen hours: withdrawn, silent, morose. Which was not like her at all, though understandable in the circumstances. Neither of them had mentioned Briggs since he had conveyed Justice's report to her; and neither of them had slept much last night, nor on the flight from Washington this morning.

When they reached the portable metal steps Augustine turned briefly to wave at the gaggle of photographers and reporters that had followed onto the station platform. Flashbulbs popped; television cameras whirred. From out at the front of the station he could hear the voices of the well-wishers who had gathered to greet him when his limousine arrived from the airport—a much smaller crowd than even on his last visit ten days ago. But that would change once he got his campaign into full swing. They would come in droves then, as they had four years ago; all over the country they would come out in droves when the Presidential Special came whistling in.

He noticed Justice standing a few feet away, looking as unobtrusive as always but with dark smudges under his eyes that said his night had also been mostly sleepless. They had exchanged but a few words this morning and none at all since leaving Washington; everything that needed to be said about Briggs had been spoken last night, and any further dialogue at this time would have been painful for both of them.

Augustine stood a moment longer, smiling impersonally for the cameras, sniffing the good oily machine odor of railroad stations everywhere. Then he turned and helped Claire up the steps, boarded after her and followed her into the corridor of U.S. Car Number One. At the door of her compartment she stopped and turned to him, putting her hand gently on his arm.

"I think I'll lie down for a while, Nicholas," she said.

"Don't you feel well?"

"I'm just tired. You ought to rest too, dear."

"I will, a little later."

She nodded, turned as Elizabeth Miller came up and asked her something about a secretarial matter. Augustine left her with Elizabeth and went up the empty corridor to his office at the far end. Just as he reached it, someone—Maxwell Harper—called his name. He sighed softly, glanced back and waited for Harper to approach him.

Maxwell had tried to get him alone at Dulles and again on Air Force One—plainly, he had something on his mind—but Augustine had been in no mood to listen to one of Harper's lectures. Nor was he now, for that matter. A brilliant man, Maxwell, but you could not interact with him on an emotional level; he thought only in terms of facts and figures, causes and effects, and dry intellectual syllogisms. It was exactly for that reason that Augustine could never tell him about the Briggs decision. Harper would be appalled by it because he would be unable to see past the act itself, would be incapable of understanding the emotions which had precipitated it.

Augustine said, "What is it, Maxwell?"

"I'd like a few minutes of your time," Harper answered in his dry precise voice.

"Everyone wants a few minutes of my time. Can't it wait?"

Harper frowned slightly. "I suppose it can, but—"

"Good. Come see me in thirty minutes or so. After we've gotten underway."

Augustine pivoted away from him, not giving him the opportunity to argue, and entered the office compartment. Facing inside, he drew the door shut behind him. When he heard Harper's steps retreating in the corridor he crossed to his desk and sank into the wide leather chair behind it.

The office was cool and dark: the Presidential Special was air conditioned, and the shades were already drawn across the windows. He sat quietly for a time, looking at the mahogany-paneled walls with their colorful display of railroad timetables and handbills and chromolithograph posters, the tufted red-velvet settee which had originally graced a Pullman drawing room on the old Erie Railroad in the 1880s, the hand-crafted bar cabinet from the Central Pacific car that had once belonged to Leland Stanford, the six-foot mahogany conference table with its satin-damask-upholstered chairs. God, it's good to be back here, he thought, and smiled to himself, and felt again the stir of excitement. There was something about trains that got into a man's blood, filled him with a sense of joy and adventure, sharpened his awareness of externals and of himself. And as he had many times before, he felt a fleeting wistful sadness that he had not ignored his father's wishes and had gone into railroading instead of politics. If he had gone into railroading, who was to say that he would not be a happier and more fulfilled man than he was today?

He began to hum "John Henry," and as soon as he did that he had a vivid mental image of a huge black man swinging a ten-pound sheep-nose hammer in the heat and the smoky darkness of a mountain tunnel in West Virginia, the Big Bend tunnel on the C&O road more than a century ago. John Henry, driving drills into bare rock to make holes for the blasting charges, risking death from silicosis and suffocation and falling rock and cave-ins, finally dying not from any of these but from sheer exhaustion in an impossible confrontation with a steam drill. John Henry, steel-driving man.

> When John Henry was a little baby,
> Sittin' on his daddy's knee,
> Point his finger at a little piece of steel,
> Say, "Hammer's gonna be the death of me,
> Lawd, Lawd," say, "Hammer's gonna be the death of me."

Augustine sang a second verse, and in the middle of a third the Presidential Special's air horn sounded to announce departure—sounded loud and harsh and toneless, nothing like those grand old whistles of yore. Humming again, he stood and went to the bar cabinet. He had wanted a drink badly last night, after Justice had first left the Oval Study, but he had restrained himself; the worst time to reach for alcohol was when you were in the middle of a crisis. But a drink or two now would not hurt. In fact, they were called for: a toast to railroading and to the memory of steel-driving men like John Henry.

While he was making himself a bourbon-and-soda, the train started to move—slowly, smoothly, the iron wheels creating small rhythmic sounds on the rails. Augustine raised his glass, drank from it, and then returned to his chair and lifted the shade on the nearest window. Outside, the network of tracks and strings of out-of-service cars slid by, shining in the hard glare of the sun; then they were gone and in their place were buildings and palm trees and the distant bluish shadows of hills and mountains.

He smiled again and sang:

> O the cap'n he told John Henry,
> "I believe this mountain's sinkin' in";
> John Henry he say to his cap'n, "O my,
> It's my hammer just a-hossin' in the wind,
> Lawd, Lawd, it's my hammer just a-hossin' in the wind."

The train picked up speed and the air horn echoed again, and Augustine experienced a familiar illusion of motionlessness, as if the Presidential Special were standing still and the world itself were rushing by. There was a curious sense of peace in that. He could imagine, at least for a while, that he had been relieved of the pressures of office, that the complexities of human society were under the influence of God alone.

He filled a pipe, settled back with it and with his drink. I wish I'd known you, John Henry, he thought. I think we'd have gotten along. Yes, by God, I think we'd have gotten along just fine.

Two

Now, here on the train as it moves away from Union Station, an understanding comes to us: the execution of Briggs was our first act of mercy, but it must not be our last.

He was only part of the conspiracy, perhaps its leader but more probably, in retrospect, its point man. There are still others involved, in any case, and before the plot can be effectively neutralized these others, too, must be eliminated. You cannot nullify a cancer by killing one of its cells; you must kill them all, every last one.

But who are they? We are not quite sure yet; we can make educated guesses, but guesses are not enough—we must be absolutely certain. Peter Kineen is a major part of the conspiracy, of course; the President, however, recognizes him as an enemy, and he is not nearly so dangerous as those close to Augustine, such as Briggs, who are seeking to undermine and destroy him from within. Kineen must die, yes, but the others, the ones still hidden, must die first.

We will be even more vigilant and cunning from now on. And when we become sure of each of the remaining traitors, we will strike as we struck with Briggs. Swiftly, vengefully, and in the name of righteousness.

Oh yes, oh yes, our acts of mercy have only just begun.

Three

Harper made his way awkwardly along the swaying corridors from the club car toward the aides' Pullman. Trains, he thought with distaste. Great lumbering anachronisms totally devoid of dignity, with no effective function in the last two decades of the twentieth century. Lower-class conveyances like buses and streetcars. Playthings for men such as Augustine who had never quite outgrown the toys and fascinations of childhood. All in all, a preposterous mode of transportation for the President of the United States, and for a man like himself whose sensibilities were offended by their superfluous nature.

The motion of the train had given him a sour stomach, and the glass of plain soda he had consumed in the club car made him belch again, delicately. He had spent fifteen minutes in the club car, brooding at one of the tables and watching flickers of sunlight play stroboscopically on its surface, but then restlessness had brought him to his feet and sent him out of there, just as it had brought him into the car in the first place.

Why had Augustine moved up the date of their departure for The Hollows from the weekend to today? Was it because of the media reaction to his ill-timed joke about the Vice-President's problems in the West? Because of the Indian crisis and his inability to cope with it? Or had something else happened, something of which Harper had not yet been made aware? The suddenness of this change in plans—Harper had learned about it only this morning, when he arrived at the White House—carried suspicious overtones. As did Augustine's refusal to talk to him in Washington and on the plane. As did the President's haggard, moody aspect. As did the First Lady's uncharacteristic reticence today, the bluish lines of fatigue under her eyes that she had not quite been able to conceal with makeup.

There were more people in the corridors now—stewards (none of whom were black: a kind of reverse racism, Harper thought ironically), other aides, and Secret Servicemen who could not quite maintain either their regimentation or their inconspicuousness in these closed surroundings. He ignored them individually, still brooding. But when he neared his compartment, at the upper end of the aides' Pullman adjacent to U.S. Car Number One, he saw through the connecting door glass that the First Lady was standing in the doorway of her private drawing room, talking to her confidential secretary, Elizabeth Miller. He hesitated, and then, on impulse, he walked through into Car Number One.

As he entered, Elizabeth Miller was saying, "Do you want me to have a steward bring us some coffee, Mrs. Augustine?" Claire nodded, started to retreat into the drawing room. Harper called, "Mrs. Augustine," and she stopped and seemed to stiffen, turning her head to look at him. Elizabeth paused, as if there was something she wanted to say to Harper, but he moved past her without a glance. He did not particularly care for the woman: she was another cipher like Justice.

His first thought as he came to Claire was that even the

marks of fatigue did not detract from her beauty. But then his eyes met hers—and what he saw reflected there reversed his smile into a startled frown.

It was something that might have been fear.

She looked past him at the secretary, said sharply, "Don't just stand there, Elizabeth, see about the coffee," and then put her eyes on him again as Elizabeth Miller left the car.

Harper began, "Mrs. Augustine—"

"I haven't time to talk now ..."

"But I was just—"

"Please, not now," she said, and before he could speak again she stepped back and pushed the door shut. Its lock clicked an instant later, like a protective barrier being snapped into place.

Nonplussed, Harper stood alone in the corridor and listened to the monotonous rhythm of the train's wheels, to the uneasy rhythm of his thoughts. Her reactions to him were sometimes mutable, yes, but never before had she seemed frightened of him. Her attitude just now made no sense. Why should she be afraid of him, of all people?

Why should she be afraid of *him?*

Four

In his small compartment in the security's Pullman, Justice sat trying to read the copy of *Murder on the Calais Coach* he had bought in Washington. And finding it dull and uninteresting. It was not the book itself, though; he knew he would have the same reaction to any mystery novel he tried to read today. After what he had done with Briggs's body last night, the fictional exploits of criminals and detectives—the imaginary dilemmas of imaginary people—took on a kind of pallid irrelevency.

Justice closed the book, rubbed at his tired eyes. Why hadn't Briggs been found? he asked himself again. He had been waiting for that to happen all day, and yet it hadn't or word would have come to the President immediately. Somebody had to find the body before long, that seemed sure: there were colleagues at the White House who would question his unexplained absence from work, friends who might investigate when appointments were not kept.

And when Briggs *was* found, what then? Had he overlooked something after all in the Cleveland Park house that would tell the homicide detectives and the forensic experts that the press secretary had not died in his bathroom? If so, would they then suspect foul play? Christ, Justice thought, that would make things even worse for the President than if they had simply reported the death at the White House. The ultimate irony: an accidental death manipulated and mishandled so badly that it was thought of as homicide.

But even if anything like that happened, the trail could lead only to him. Where it would end because he would never reveal the truth, would never betray the President or his oath of silence.

Justice raised the novel again, looked at the spine, and then tossed it onto the seat opposite without reopening it. He wondered if he should go out of there, find something or someone to occupy his time and his mind. A drink in the club car, or a predinner snack from the buffet in the dining car, or a nap, or a look at the view from the observation platform, or conversation with some of the other Secret Service agents. Only none of these things appealed to him. He did not feel like doing anything at all.

After a time he slid over next to the window, watched inanimate objects appear and disappear outside as the train sped northeast out of Los Angeles. Even the pleasure he usually felt at being on the Presidential Special was absent; he was merely riding on a transportation vehicle, like Air Force One earlier, that was taking him from one point to another. Taking all of them to The Hollows again as it had so many times in the past.

When would Briggs be found?

Had he overlooked something in the Cleveland Park house that would make the police suspect foul play?

And the fear that had been born last night remained lodged like a bone inside him. The fear that did not yet have a name.

Five

There was a light but insistent rapping on the office door.

Augustine was on his feet, about to approach the bar cabinet again because he had finished his drink and decided to permit himself a refill. He frowned as the knocking continued. Maxwell already? Well all right, he might as well get that over with; he felt relaxed enough now to deal with a lecture, if that was what Harper intended to deliver.

He went to the door and drew it open. But it was not Harper who stood outside.

It was Julius Wexford.

Augustine stared at him, unable to understand for an instant how Wexford could be here. When he had thought at all about the attorney general in the past forty-eight hours, he had had him compartmentalized with the National Committee in Saint Louis. And Wexford had not been at Union Station in Los Angeles when Augustine boarded the train; he must have arrived afterward, just before departure.

"Hello, Nicholas," Wexford said gravely. His suit was

rumpled and he had a harried, bleak-eyed look about him. But there was none of the nervousness he had shown two days ago in the Oval Office; his florid face was dry and his eyes were steady and resolute. "You seem surprised to see me."

"That's putting it mildly."

"May I come in?"

"I suppose you might as well."

Augustine moved aside to let him enter, reclosed the door. Wexford glanced at the red-velvet settee, glanced at the empty glass the President held, and then stood as if waiting for an invitation to sit down, an offer of a drink. Augustine gave him neither. Instead he went to his desk, set the glass down on it, rested a hip against its outer edge, and folded his arms across his chest.

"All right, Julius," he said, "what are you doing here?"

"I received word early this morning that you were on your way to California, so I took the first available plane out of Saint Louis."

"That doesn't answer my question."

"There are things that have to be resolved," Wexford said. "Now, not whenever you decide to return to Washington."

"Cabinet business?"

"No. You know perfectly well what things I mean."

"I gave you my decision on Wednesday," Augustine said. He could feel his nerves tightening again. "The issue is closed."

The gentle sway of the train seemed to bother Wexford; he was prone, Augustine knew, to mild motion sickness. He backed over to the settee and sat on it with his hands splayed out on both sides of him, as though bracing himself. "I wonder if you realize," he said solemnly, "just how much trouble we're in right now."

"*We're* in?"

"Yes. You, me, all of us in the party."

"The way I see it, the only ones in trouble are you and

your friends. I'd fire you right now, publicly, except that an open split won't do me any good. When I'm reelected I intend to make that my first priority."

"You're not going to be reelected, Nicholas, because you're not going to be renominated."

"Oh yes I am. I'm in better shape than Johnson was in 1968 and *he* would have been renominated. I'm in infinitely better shape than Truman was in 1948 and he *won*. An incumbent president can't be denied the renomination of his own party if he wants it badly enough. And I want it that badly."

"You're not going to get it," Wexford said. He took a heavy breath. "I won't mince words this time; I'll just give you the hard-line truth. You're losing credibility faster than any president in history, including Nixon. The media is saying it and the polls show it. In the past few weeks you've mishandled domestic affairs, you've lost all perspective on foreign policy and managed to alienate the Israelis and the Jewish electorate and to embarrass the Vice-President, and you come out here to California two or three times a month like Nixon in his last days running off to Key Biscayne or San Clemente. There's no indication that you're even maintaining an appearance of the presidency any longer. You're harming the country and destroying yourself politically, and that's bad enough; but you're also dragging the party down with you, jeopardizing the careers of dozens of good men who are up for national and state reelection in five months."

Bile burned in Augustine's throat; he felt himself trembling. "That's quite a speech," he said thinly.

"I'm sorry, Nicholas, but it had to be said. You're a decent man and for most of your term you've been viable. But you're not the same person you were even six months ago. I hate to say this, but you seem to be suffering from some sort of mental deterioration and plunging toward a complete neurasthenic collapse—"

"Bullshit."

Wexford looked down at his hands. "I'm sorry, Nicholas, but that's the way it looks to me and to a lot of others."

"Is that all you have to say?"

"No, I'm afraid it isn't," Wexford said, and raised his eyes again. "The point of all this is that the National Committee has decided—unanimously—to ask for party unity behind Kineen and there's not much doubt now that we'll be able to get it. There are quite a few angry people in this administration."

"So you're here to demand an immediate statement of withdrawal," Augustine said. "Demand it, not ask for it."

"We'd settle for that, yes."

"Settle for it?"

"The party wants you to resign," Wexford said.

Augustine went rigid.

Wexford said quickly, "It would turn public opinion around, you must see that. You'd go out on an act of strength and courage, you'd create sympathy and respect and you'd give the party the leverage we need to mend fences, restore confidence and put Kineen in the White House. Conroy is an intelligent man, he won't have any difficulty assuming Executive matters until—"

"You son of a bitch," Augustine said, "how dare you come onto my train and accuse me of heading toward a mental breakdown and then tell me to resign? How dare you tell me I'm not fit to continue as President of the United States?"

"Nicholas ..."

Augustine came forward until he was standing two feet from Wexford, towering over him. Intimidated, Wexford drew back; he moistened his lips and put a hand up and started to speak.

Furiously Augustine cut him off. "Don't you think I understand what's really behind all this? The media starts blowing statements and actions all out of proportion, the polls reflect a temporary confusion among the populace, and right away front-runners like you begin believing things are going downhill because I'm losing control. You convince yourselves I'm to blame for *all* the country's troubles and *all* the party's troubles, and the only hope is for me to resign or at least to withdraw. Throw me to the wolves, let them feed on my bones, and meanwhile it's business as usual. Who the hell cares if my good name and my career die in ignominy? Who the hell cares if everything I've tried to do and have done winds up in ashes just so long as the goddamn party can run a whitewash?"

Wexford struggled to his feet, backed two steps away from Augustine. "That's not true," he said. "None of that is true—"

"It's true, all right, and I'm not going to sit still for it. You hear me? I won't resign, I won't withdraw. You go back to Saint Louis tomorrow and tell them that—first thing tomorrow, right after we arrive at The Hollows station. I don't want you at the ranch; I don't want to see you anywhere except in Washington on urgent cabinet matters. Is that clear?"

Tight-lipped, Wexford said, "I'm warning you, Nicholas, if you keep on this way you'll wind up broken and humiliated."

"We'll just see about that."

"It will happen," Wexford said grimly, "because it'll be all gloves off. If you force us to take harsh measures to keep the party in power, we're prepared to do it."

"Are you threatening me, Julius?"

"No. I'm just telling you you mustn't and you won't be renominated. For the good of all of us."

"Personalities, smear tactics?" Augustine said. "Would you really go that far?"

"I hope to God you don't make me find out." Wexford

turned to the door, opened it, stepped out into the corridor. "I'll be in my compartment if you want to talk again after you've calmed down a little—"

Augustine caught the door and slammed it shut.

Bastard, he thought. Bastard! And went immediately to the bar cabinet to pour himself another drink.

Six

Harper let a full forty minutes pass before he left his compartment and went again to the President's office. When he knocked on the satinwood panel there were several seconds of silence, and then Augustine's voice said thickly, "Who is it?"

"Maxwell."

Another few moments of silence. "All right, come on in. The door's open."

Harper entered. The office was dark, but an elongation of light from the corridor reached across to where Augustine sat behind his desk. He had both elbows propped on the blotter and he was holding the stem from one of his pipes up in front of the window, peering through it as though it were a telescope. There was a glass of whiskey in front of him and his cheeks were flushed, peppered with flecks of perspiration. He looked tense and angry.

Harper's edginess increased as he closed the door. First the sudden decision to leave for California, then Claire's inexplicable behavior a little while ago, and now Augustine looking as though something had disturbed him since they'd last spoken. The crisis and the way it kept escalating was bad enough, but at least he could deal with that on an intellectual level; it was the undercurrents, the dark and hidden complexities that seemed to be developing, which worried him most.

Augustine lowered the pipe stem, picked up the glass instead and sipped from it. Then he made a face, appeared to shudder, and took his elbows off the desk and set the glass down again. He fixed Harper with a slightly bleary look. "Well, Maxwell?"

Harper took a chair opposite the desk. "I'd like to know," he said slowly, "why you decided to come to The Hollows today."

"I told you that in Washington. I need a few days' rest."

"Yes, but you also told me you planned to leave on Sunday. Why did you move it up two days?"

"Do I have to have specific reasons for everything I do? I'm in California because I want to be in California."

"But it's a matter of timing. The media—"

"Damn the media! I'm sick unto death of the media."

"We all are," Harper said. "But that's not the point. The point is that you've further jeopardized your position for no good reason that I can see. Or *is* there a reason, something you're keeping from me? You've been acting strangely all day."

For a moment, lips pursed, Augustine stared at him with sudden enmity; but then it seemed to fade from his eyes—or into them, like something sinking in dark water—until they were clear again. He picked up his glass but did not drink from it, only peered at the dark liquid as if searching for something within its depths.

"I have nothing to tell you about my moods or my private decisions," he said. "There are some things I choose not to share with even my closest advisors; you understand that, I hope."

I do not understand it, Harper thought. He watched the President take another sip of whiskey. "Will you at least tell me why you're drinking so much at this time of day?"

"It happens to be five o'clock. The cocktail hour."

"You've had more than one or two drinks."

"And what if I have? I don't have to justify my drinking habits to you, do I?"

"I suppose you don't," Harper said stiffly.

Augustine made an abrupt slicing gesture with one hand. "Oh all right," he said, "you might as well know. You'd find it out anyway before long."

"Find what out?"

"Wexford is here on the train," the President said. "He flew out to Los Angeles this afternoon and came aboard just before we left. I finished talking to him not ten minutes ago."

Harper's hands clenched. "Why did he come?"

"A goddamn search-and-destroy mission, that's why."

"Don't give me metaphors, Nicholas—"

"He wants my resignation," Augustine said. Matter-of-factly, as if he were delivering an irritating but not particularly important bit of news. "On behalf of the National Committee and the party-at-large. They're not requesting now, they're issuing ultimatums."

My God, Harper thought. Oh my God. . . .

Seven

Elizabeth.

Yes, Mrs. Augustine?

Are you familiar with the twenty-fifth amendment?

To the Constitution?

That's right.

I know what it says, yes.

What does it say?

Well, it empowers the President to nominate a successor if the Vice-President should die or resign from office. And it stipulates what's to be done if the President himself should die or be incapacitated. But you know that as well as I do, Mrs. Augustine.

Yes. How long has it been since you read it closely?

Not since college. Why are you asking me about the twenty-fifth amendment?

This is really terrible coffee. I can't understand why the kitchen staff can't make better coffee.

Mrs. Augustine, why did you ask me about the twenty-fifth amendment?

I was just thinking of Vice-President Conroy, that's all. He has a weak heart, you know, and there are reports that he's been having palpitations after what happened in Phoenix. I understand he's returning to Washington and will be checking into Walter Reed for a few days.

Oh, I hope it's nothing serious.

So do I. But it gives one pause to reflect.

It does, doesn't it. Would you like me to have the kitchen make you a fresh pot of coffee?

No, I've had enough coffee. I think I'll lie down again. I shouldn't have asked you in again; we haven't anything to do that can't wait until we get to The Hollows.

You do look exhausted, Mrs. Augustine. Haven't you been sleeping well?

Not very well, no. I've had insomnia.

You should have seen Doctor Whiting and had him give you something.

Maybe you're right, Elizabeth. Yes, I should have seen Doctor Whiting. Elizabeth?

Yes?

Draw those window shades, would you, before you leave? It's much too bright in here. Much too bright.

Eight

Justice entered the dining car a few minutes before eight and took a seat at an empty table at the far end. The car was less than half full, mostly with staff aides and a few Secret Servicemen; white-jacketed waiters glided along the center aisle, balancing trays and silver ice buckets and bottles of California wine. Conversation was muted, and there was none of the relaxed camaraderie, the easy laughter, which normally prevailed at dinnertime on the Presidential Special. The faces of the diners were as sober as they had been on the flight from Washington; it was obvious that each of them, too, was deeply concerned about the negative trend of recent events.

A pitcher of ice water stood on the table. Justice poured some into a glass, drank a little of it and then opened the menu that lay across the place setting in front of him. Crabmeat cocktail, Crenshaw melon, liver pâté; roast beef, abalone steak, chicken baked in wine sauce; salad and vegetables; strawberries in cream or three different kinds of cheese. A good selection—but none of it appealed to him. He closed the menu again, put it aside. He was simply not hungry.

When a waiter appeared beside him Justice ordered a cup of coffee. Then he sat staring out the near window. Green and brown farmland now; fields of alfalfa and lettuce and tomatoes. The sun had dipped behind the mountains of the Coastal Range, and the sky was suffused with a fading brick-red glow that turned scattered cloud wisps into stark luminous streaks, like designs in an abstract painting. But it all had a hypnotic effect on him, as had the scenery he'd observed from his compartment window, and when he felt his thoughts turning introspective again he shook himself and looked away.

The waiter arrived with his coffee. There was nothing to hold his attention while he drank it, and after a time he lifted the copy of *Murder on the Calais Coach* that he had brought with him and tried once more to read.

He had managed to absorb two full pages when he sensed someone standing close by, watching him. He glanced up, and it was Maxwell Harper.

Harper wore a sardonic expression, and his eyes were as hard and shiny as polished opals. He stood in the aisle with arms akimbo, swaying slightly to the motion of the train. "Hello, Justice," he said. "Mind if I join you?"

Reluctantly Justice said, "No sir, not at all."

Harper sat down across from him. A waiter appeared immediately, but Harper gestured him away and watched as Justice closed the book and laid it to one side of his cup. "A mystery story," he said. "I might have known that was the kind of thing you'd read."

"Sir?"

"Oh, no offense," Harper said neutrally. "Lots of people read them. The President himself, as long as they have railroad backgrounds. Like Roosevelt with pulp westerns and Kennedy with James Bond spy novels."

"Yes sir."

Harper shrugged. "Personally I find popular fiction dull and totally lacking in literary merit and intelligent ideas. A soporific rather than a stimulant."

Justice said nothing.

"How do you feel about it?" Harper asked.

"Sir?"

"Popular fiction. Do you think it has literary merit?"

"I really couldn't say. I don't know much about things like that."

"Well do you find mysteries intellectually stimulating?"

"Sometimes. Mostly I read them for entertainment."

"So you have no real opinion on them."

"No."

Harper folded his arms on the table and leaned against them. "Just what do you have opinions on, Justice? You can't be as dull-witted as that face of yours indicates."

Justice wondered if all of this was intended as some sort of sly game: the intellectual feeding his ego by putting down someone he obviously considered to be inferior. Or was there more to it than that? He had been aware for some time that Harper felt a certain hostility toward him, though he could never quite understand why. Maybe this was Harper's way of working out his frustrations and aggressions. At any rate, Justice decided he could endure it; Harper was close to the President, a trusted advisor, and that was all that really mattered.

"Well?" Harper said.

"I guess I don't have many opinions at all, Mr. Harper."

"Not even on political matters?"

"No sir."

"Oh come now. You must have views on the current situation—Briggs, Oberdorfer, Wexford, the press reaction to the President's comments on Israel and the Vice-President."

"My views are the President's views," Justice said.

"Just a member of the flock following his shepherd." Harper's expression grew even more sardonic. "All right, I'll accept that. But what about some of the issues of the day? The balance of power, for instance. Do you think there has been a reconstitution of the essential power structure preceding the Second World War with the *ex-post facto* difference that Israel may now ironically be said to be in the position of the Axis powers? By which I mean, disregarding ideology and spiritual mysticism, that Israel is in effect holding the world hostage to the possibility of violence on an ever-larger scale. Is that how you see it, Justice?"

Justice blinked at him. "I'm afraid I don't understand."

"No? Well, perhaps you feel that there has been an irreparable shift in *all* power relationships, that they must be exposed to entirely different definitions. In that case we are not talking about culture lag but culture shock, the distinguished theories of Emile Durkheim notwithstanding. Is cultural lag being obliterated? Or simply reaugmented?"

"Mr. Harper," Justice said, "I just don't understand what you're saying."

"No, I can see you don't, at that. Well suppose we try something a little less complex and more to the point."

"Point of what, sir?"

"Julius Wexford," Harper said.

"Sir?"

"Why the blank look? Don't tell me you haven't talked to the President in the past couple of hours? I was under the impression he discussed everything of any consequence with you lately."

Justice said, "I haven't talked to him at all since we boarded the train," and then frowned and asked, "Has something happened, Mr. Harper?"

"Certainly something has happened. The President and Wexford had a confrontation earlier this afternoon."

Justice was momentarily confused. "You mean here, on the Presidential Special? I thought Mr. Wexford was in Saint Louis . . ."

"So did we all," Harper said. "The fact is, he came on

behalf of the National Committee—to demand the President's resignation."

Stunned, Justice said, "Resignation?"

"You heard me; I don't need to repeat myself."

"But why?"

"That should be obvious even to you," Harper said. "They're afraid he has lost enough credibility to destroy the party at the polls in November; they want to sweep him out so they can quote reestablish public faith unquote and elect Peter Kineen in his place."

"Mr. Wexford said this to the President?"

"That, and a great deal more. Augustine believes him to be the guiding force behind the movement against him. Along with Kineen, of course."

"Then he didn't agree to the demand—?"

"Of course not. He intends to fight; he still believes he can win renomination."

"Can he?" Justice asked softly.

"It hardly looks promising. The National Committee plans to mount an all-out campaign for Kineen's nomination, which means there will be strong in-party attacks on the President as well as vicious opposition attacks. His credibility is liable to plummet even further, and if that happens even his staunchest backers will abandon him for fear of losing their jobs to Kineen partisans. And those of us who are too deeply committed to the President to effectively switch sides will suffer even more; the party will excommunicate us, we'll never work in government again at a national or even a state level."

Justice felt cold. "Isn't there anything that can be done, Mr. Harper? Isn't there any way to make Mr. Wexford and the National Committee reconsider?"

"That, Justice," Harper said, "is a damned good question. *The* question, in fact."

"Sir?"

"It's the reason I'm here talking to you."

"I don't understand . . ."

"For Christ's sake, are you really as dense as all that? I've been sitting in my compartment for the past three hours trying to come up with a solution, a plan, a viable counter-measure. Much as it pains me to admit it, I'm stymied. And the reason for that may be that I attack a problem from the intellectual point of view and what is needed here is a more direct and basic approach. Do you understand now?"

"You want my help?" Justice said, astonished.

"I want an opinion from you, damn it." Anger—or maybe a kind of self-deprecating embarrassment—shone in Harper's eyes. "Come on, Justice, you're as involved in this as I am; the President has seen to that. Tell me what the common man, the man of action, thinks ought to be done."

Justice shook his head. He understood just how grave the situation must be for a proud, aloof genius such as Harper to come seeking help from someone such as himself. But he had no alternative answers to offer; his mind was as blank in this moment as an erased slateboard. "I don't know, sir," he said. "I just . . . I don't know."

Harper gave him a look of disgust, got abruptly to his feet. "Behold the common man, the product of two centuries of struggle and pain since the French Revolution—totally incapable of creative thought or action."

"I want to help, Mr. Harper," Justice said, "but I don't know how. I'm not a thinker or a planner, I'm just a man who follows orders—"

But Harper had already turned and was walking away.

Nine

And now we are sure of another one, a second part of the conspiracy, a second cell of the cancer which must be destroyed. He has been a major suspect all along, of course, especially for the past few days, but still there is an element of shock in unmistakable knowledge. The truth is always difficult, revelation carries its own small clout of pain, because for a long time we trusted him, we believed in him, and it is always painful to come face to face with deceit and your own misjudgments.

But that is not important. All that is important is that he is a traitor. The evidence is damning, the verdict is in, and sentence has been passed: he is a traitor, and he must die.

Tonight.

He must be executed tonight ...

Ten

Dinner in Claire's drawing room: the two of them alone, the lights turned down and a pair of slim tapers burning in silver holders, good cuisine and a good bottle of estate-bottled pinot chardonnay, the wind whispering beyond the shaded windows and combining with the steady hum of the train wheels to form a kind of muted background music, Claire in a sheer white dressing gown and with her hair brushed into long smooth waves the way he liked her to wear it.

All the ingredients were there, Augustine thought, but the dinner was not what it could have been, what it should have been on the Presidential Special. There was no intimacy, no sense of peace or contentment. Claire seemed rested tonight, after her nap, but she was still quiet and withdrawn; and he was nearly exhausted and his head ached from the bourbon he had drunk too much of and his mind kept working, working, stuttering from one thought to another. They had said little to each other, and yet there was a strained atmosphere that seemed to linger between them, as if Claire had difficult things to say to him just as he had difficult things to say to her. Which made the dinner little more than an excuse for delay.

Augustine picked at his roast beef and watched her across the table. She had stopped eating—had barely touched her food anyway—and was looking now into her wine glass. Her eyes were dark, unreadable, somewhat distant; she looked in that aspect to be deep in a kind of spiritual meditation. In the flickering light from the candle flames her face had a distinctive, almost haunting beauty, like that of a woman seen and coveted but never known.

At length he put down his own fork, dabbed at his mouth with the linen napkin. Might as well get it over with, he thought. He cleared his throat.

Claire blinked, focused on him again. "Yes, Nicholas?"

"There's something you should know," he said, "something that happened this afternoon."

A soft sigh. "About Julius Wexford, you mean."

"You know he's here on board?"

"Yes. He came to see me after he spoke to you."

"Oh he did, did he. Then I suppose he told you about the National Committee's decision."

"I'm afraid so."

So the difficult things plaguing both of them were the same. He ran a hand through his hair. "What else did he say?"

"He begged me to ask you to reconsider."

"I'll bet he did. For my sake and for the sake of the party and the country—is that how he put it?"

"Yes."

"Did he also tell you he thinks I'm deteriorating mentally, heading for a breakdown?"

She winced. "Yes."

"And what did you say?"

"I told him I didn't want to listen to that kind of talk. I told him I found his and the National Committee's opinions distasteful and their tactics unforgivable. If they had met with you personally, been frank and open with you instead of going behind your back—"

"It wouldn't have made any difference," Augustine said. He studied her closely. "Damn it, Claire, you didn't let him convince you my position is as hopeless as they claim."

"I didn't let him convince me of anything."

"But you think it just might be hopeless, don't you."

"Nothing is hopeless," she said.

"That doesn't answer my question."

"Nicholas, it's just that with party unity behind Kineen, you're facing an awesome struggle—a vicious and painful one—and I can't help but worry what it might do to you."

"It won't do anything to me except put me back in the White House for another four years. We're going to beat them, Claire, I promise you that. Together we're going to beat them."

Claire rotated her wine glass, silent.

"Together," he said again.

"Yes," she said, "together."

Augustine nodded. "We'll begin the campaign as soon as we return to Washington. I've got several ideas on how to proceed. But the first thing is to appoint a new campaign chairman and I've been thinking about Ed Dougherty. How do you feel about him?"

"He might be a good choice, yes."

"Then again, maybe Maxwell Harper would be an even better one."

"No," Claire said immediately.

"Well, he's a brilliant man. In the past his advice—"

"I don't want to hear about Maxwell's advice," she said, and there was a vehemence in her voice that surprised him. "I don't care about his advice. I don't want you even to consider him as a campaign chairman."

"Why not? My God, you sound as though you no longer like or trust him."

"I don't."

"But why?"

"Nicholas, please. Let's just drop the subject of Maxwell Harper."

"All right," he said. "For now. But I just don't understand this sudden animosity toward him."

She was silent again.

Frowning, Augustine massaged his temples. "Do you want to hear my ideas for the campaign?"

"Wouldn't you rather rest now? You hardly slept last night and you look exhausted. You can tell me your ideas at The Hollows."

"Maybe you're right," he said. "Maybe I should get to bed right away." He paused. "Do you want to join me?"

"A little later, if you'd like."

"I would. I'd prefer not to sleep alone tonight."

He stood and stepped around to kiss her. Then he went to the connecting door between their compartments, opened it and stepped through. Before he reshut the door he looked at her again. The candlelight played across the soft planes of her face—and he was struck once more by the haunting beauty of her in that aspect, by the vaguely unsettling feeling that even after twenty years of marriage, he did not really know her at all.

The feeling stayed with him even after he was in bed and waiting for sleep to come and carry him away.

Eleven

Restless, unable to sleep, Harper paced the floor of his compartment in small widening circles, returning to the center of the room when the circles increased enough to bring him up against walls and furnishings. He tended to do that when he was brooding, perhaps because it was an objective correlative for the way in which his mind worked: begin at the center, forage outward from a central idea or conception.

But the pacing did him little more good now than it had earlier. He still could not come up with an effective strategy for counteracting the crisis. And he still could not find answers to the hidden aspects of it, to the strange behavior of Claire and the reticence of the President.

He berated himself again, yet again, for going to Justice and humbling himself in front of the man. It had been a foolish error in judgment, a lapse in the strict control by which he lived and functioned. He had succeeded in doing nothing except demean himself. How could he have thought that a cipher like Justice could contribute anything in the way of positive action if he himself could not?

Well, it was a measure of his frustration and his apprehension, he supposed. Apprehension not only for Augustine but for himself; *his* career was as much on the line as was the President's.

His career. A doctorate in political science from Harvard, four years at the Institute of Policy Studies, twelve years on the faculty at Harvard and then the Wilson chair at Northwestern, the Pulitzer Prize nomination for his biography of Millard Fillmore, and finally his appointment as domestic affairs advisor. No small accomplishments, any of these. And yet he had always considered his greatest achievements to lie ahead of him: the contributions he would eventually make, not only politically but to history and to American letters, would be the true realization of his capabilities.

But now it seemed probable that his future held little more than bitter unfulfillment and the relative anonymity of the vanquished. That he would be overtaken by that very history which should have enshrined him. And all because he had made the one fatal error of tying himself too tightly to a man he had believed strong but who had turned out to be weak. And vulnerable.

The unfairness of it was galling.

And I can't let it happen, he told himself grimly. I must not let it happen. In that sense he was like Augustine: unable to give up, unable under any circumstances to passively accept defeat. It was a matter of honor and dignity and pride, a matter of utter belief in the rightness of himself and his role in the power structure of government.

So he would fight. He would stand behind the President and fight, and maybe, just maybe, they could win the struggle. Would win it, *had* to win it. There had to be ways to find answers to muddled equations, ways to turn things around.

Harper stopped pacing, stood listening to the rumbling clatter of the train. The compartment was beginning to have a claustrophobic effect on him, he realized; it preyed on his senses, made him irritable and dulled his thought processes. And perhaps he was spending too much time alone in here; perhaps he ought to get out and *do* something instead of pacing around and thinking about something to do. Talk to the President again? No, not tonight. Tomorrow would be better, after Augustine had had a night's sleep and was more alert and less inclined to be emotional.

Talk to Wexford?

Yes, he thought, Wexford. A calm, rational discussion. Find out just how strong party sentiment was against the President; find out if there were any compromises that could be made. Find some sort of direction. That was what he should have done in the first place, for God's sake, instead of stupidly seeking out Justice.

Quickly Harper left the compartment and went in search of the attorney general.

Twelve

In the night Augustine awoke and for a disoriented moment did not know where he was. Then he heard the smooth comforting rhythm of the train wheels, and the faint contrapuntal rhythm of the wind outside and of Claire's breathing beside him, and the confusion passed and left him dully aware of his surroundings.

He shifted position on the berth so that he was lying on his back. What had awakened him? A dream, perhaps, although he could not remember dreaming; a sudden lurch as the Presidential Special negotiated a curve; a sound penetrating from somewhere in the night. Whatever it was, it was not important. What was important was recapturing sleep, the good deep sleep he had fallen into before Claire joined him and then again afterward. He reclosed his eyes, turned his cheek into the pillow.

But sleep did not come at all this time.

He waited a long while for it and it did not come.

He lay poised on the rim of consciousness, listening to the train, feeling the sway of it and its faint vibrations in the mattress beneath him. Gentle, insistent, throbbing. Throbbing. An assault both on the body and on the senses. Throb-and-sway. Throb-and sway . . .

It gave him an erection.

Not all at once but in small pulsing surges—and he lay still, expecting it to diminish and leave him flaccid again. Instead the surges increased until the erection was complete. A dim elation moved through him. His first full erection in weeks, and one as achingly rigid as any he had had in the viril days of his youth. The sensations in his groin were exquisite.

In careful movements he turned onto his side and put a hand on Claire's warm hip. "Claire," he whispered. "Claire?"

She moaned softly but did not wake up.

Augustine tugged his pajama bottoms down, freeing himself, and then drew Claire's gown up over her buttocks. She stirred, lifting her body to help him, but in a reflexive way that told him she was still asleep. He rolled the gown over her stomach and above her breasts, moved close to her and raised her leg atop his thigh, turning and fitting her body tightly to his, pressing against the warmth of her abdomen.

He caressed her, kissed the pulsebeat in the hollow of her throat. The sensations grew demanding, and when he lowered a hand to touch her he felt that she, too, was ready. He said her name again—and entered her.

She made another moaning sound, one which seemed to him to be approving, but he could not see her face in the darkness, could not tell if her eyes had come open.

He began to move within her, consciously setting his rhythm to that of the train. Throb. Sway. Her hips answered his movements, matched them in perfect unity, and he heard the tempo of her breathing increase; when he said her name yet another time, though, she did not answer. He clutched at her breasts, traced his lips along the line of her jaw. Urgency spiraled inside him, and the thrust of his hips became more rapid, and all around him the train hummed and vibrated.

Throb, sway, throb sway, throbsway, throbsway throbsway throbswaythrobswaythrobsway . . .

Orgasm overtook him, intense and ecstatic, wringing soft cries from him and from Claire. It seemed to last a long time, so long that it approached the level of pain. When it finally ebbed his body spasmed once and went lax; he lay quiescent, they both lay quiescent, still joined, and he felt languor flowing through him in slow gentle sweeps.

Good, he thought fuzzily, it was really good again.

Then the languor deepened and he began to drift on it and on the motion of the train, and after a while he slept. And dreamed about Briggs and a coffin being lowered into the ground in Arlington Cemetery amid a circle of laughing faces. The dream was unsettling, despite its lack of detail or cohesion; he withdrew from it in stages, like someone backing slowly out of a dark movie theater—

—until he was awake again.

There was no disorientation this time; he was immediately aware of where he was, and of the fact that he was once more lying on his back, no longer touching Claire. The darkness in the compartment was heavy, complete except for faint shadow images dancing on the walls: reflections of passing landscape filtered through the partially shaded windows. Augustine turned his head to look at Claire, saw her as a dim silhouette beneath the blankets. He reached out to touch her hip again, felt the sleek material of her gown instead of bare flesh, and then realized that his own pajama bottoms were snug around his waist.

He could not remember having pulled them up. Had Claire done that for him? On impulse, he put his face close to hers. She was also resting on her back, mouth open, making faint snoring sounds; the position of her body, Augustine thought, was almost exactly as it had been after she had come into the berth with him.

Looking at her, he felt a sudden unease. What if she had not, after all, come awake during the time he was making love to her? What if she failed in the morning to bear witness to his success, even questioned that it had happened at all? What if she considered it a kind of wish-fulfilling dream on his part?

What if she was right?

The thought was abrupt and jarring. He rejected it instantly—and yet, while he recalled the sensations of the act clearly, the physical details were blurred, as in a memory of something which took place long ago. As in a dream—

The sensations.

He slid a hand beneath the covers, touched the front of his pajamas. And felt dampness, a faint stickiness. No, he thought, not at my age, not after all those nights of failure.

But it was true and he knew it.

A dream. It had all been nothing more than a wet dream . . .

Thirteen

Justice sat in his dark compartment and told himself he ought to go to bed, get some sleep, because it was after midnight now and he would have to be up at six. But he did not move, only continued to look out the window at the black shapes of mountains and cutbanks and tree-covered ridges: the Presidential Special was moving now through the foothills of the Sierra Nevada, somewhere northeast of Stockton. High running clouds obscured the moon and part of the sky, but stars winked here and there like tiny watching eyes.

There's just nothing I can do, he thought. Mr. Harper shouldn't have come to me, he shouldn't have tried to put any of the burden on me. It's not *up* to me, I'm just a Secret Service bodyguard, a civil servant with no authority and no influence. What can I do to help the President that I haven't already done?

He kept on sitting there, watching the eyes in the sky that seemed to be watching him.

Fourteen

The observation car is empty when we come into it from the club car, but through the door-window opposite we can see the dark silhouette of a man standing outside on the platform, the red-embered tip of a cigar like a hole burning in the darkness beside him. Wexford? It must be, we think. We have been to his compartment in one of the forward cars and found it empty, and we have not located him anywhere else on the train.

We cross to the door, slide it open. Cold night air surges against our face, spiced with the fragrance of spruce and pine, and the magnified clacking hum of steel on steel buffets our ears. The man at the far railing turns, and in the outspill of light behind us we can see him plainly. The muted thunder of the wheels seems to lift into a throbbing, wailing cadence, like a voice in the night.

Wex-ford, Wex-ford, Wex-ford . . .

We close the door, walk over next to him at the railing.

He is wearing an overcoat buttoned to the throat and his hair is rumpled from the wind. Night-shadowed, his florid face has a waxy cast. He does not look dangerous, he only looks old and meek, like a benign grandfather. False illusion. We know him for what he really is, and our hatred for him glows as bright as the tip of his last cigar.

"Oh," he says, "it's you."

"Yes," we say. Like him, we have raised our voice in order to be heard above the chanting of the wheels.

"Train upsets my stomach so I can't sleep," he says. "I thought some fresh air might help. Couldn't you sleep either?"

"No. Not yet, anyway. Not for a while."

"It's pretty cold out here. You ought to have a coat."

"I don't mind the cold. It's the heat that bothers me."

"Heat?"

"Yes," we say, "the heat."

Wexford frowns slightly, raises his cigar and draws on it until the tip shimmers cherry red and the wind strips away its dead ash. We can see the glow of it reflected in his eyes.

The car lurches as the train moves into a long curve and we put out a hand to grasp the rail. Our fingers brush the back of Wexford's hand; we jerk them away because we do not want to touch him, not that way. As we look at him his mouth puckers and his throat works—a silent belch, as if the sudden lurch-and-sway has made him nauseous. He peers distastefully at his cigar, then flicks it out over the railing where the wind catches it and hurls it into the night amid a shower of sparks. His mouth opens and we watch him breathe deeply several times.

Then we say, "You don't like trains, do you?"

"No. I never have."

"They're an integral part of American history, you know."

"I suppose so."

"Just like treachery," we say.

That startles him. "What?"

"There have been traitors in Washington for two hundred years," we say calmly. "You're not the first and you won't be the last."

"Exactly what is that supposed to mean?"

"You know what it means. You're a traitor, Julius—just as Briggs was. But you're even worse because you've hidden your treachery behind a mask of friendship and personal trust."

He glares at us, his mouth pinched with aggrieved anger. "What kind of wild talk is that?" he says. "I won't stand for it."

We shrug. "The truth is always painful."

"I demand an apology."

"Demand all you like."

He stands flustered, at a loss for words. "We'll see about this," he says finally, and starts to move past us.

The voice of the train says, *Wex-ford, Wex-ford, Wex-ford.*

We look back through the door-window; the observation car is still empty. In the darkness, then, we take from our jacket pocket one of the train's standard White House heavy glass ashtrays which we had picked up in our compartment. We cup it upside down in our palm, holding it along our hip where he cannot see it.

"We have a little something to make you sleep," we say.

He hesitates, half-turning toward us. "What's that?"

"To make you sleep," we say again, and we thrust the ashtray straight up against the bridge of his nose with such force that pain erupts in our armpit and chest.

A sharp cracking thud, a gasp that strangulates almost instantly in his throat. Wexford's hands flutter up toward his face, spasm, then fall limply as his legs give way and he drops bull-like to his knees. We sidestep quickly, watch him topple over against the railing and lie still, lie silent.

Lie dead.

Another execution, another act of mercy completed.

We check the observation car another time, but no one has come inside in the past few seconds. Then we hurl the ashtray into the night, bend to grasp Wexford under the arms. In death his features seem to have softened, to have lost form and definition like gray wax melting. The skin of his face is cold against our bare wrist; but we don't mind it now because we are not touching *him*, we are only touching a lifeless shell.

He is much heavier than Briggs was and it takes us a minute or two of straining effort to lift him across the railing so that most of his bulk is tipped forward and hanging down toward the tracks below. We step back then and take his ankles, heave up once, push once—and he slides away from us and is gone.

We lean forward on the railing, trying to see where he has landed. We seem to see him bounce and roll across the tracks, off the right-of-way, but the train is moving so rapidly and the night is so dark that we cannot be sure. Not that it matters. On or off the tracks, he'll be found eventually by searchers; this is not a wilderness area of gorges and deep ravines that might hide forever the body of an old traitor. The main thing is, his death, too, will appear to have been a tragic accident.

The wind is chill on our face, but it is also somehow soothing; we continue to stand looking down at the black steel ribbons appearing and retreating beneath us—so close beneath us that we imagine we can reach down and touch them. The voice of the wheels shrieks in our ears, only we realize abruptly that it is no longer saying *Wex-ford*. We close our eyes, listening.

And the words become clear. *You-too*, the train is saying now. *You-too, you-too, you-too*.

We do not find this strange, nor does it frighten us. We have thought of suicide before: the utter peace of death is appealing. But this is not the time or the place, and we do not want to lie out there with Julius. We must continue to be strong until the conspiracy has been completely and irrevocably destroyed.

We stop listening to the wheels and turn for the door.

Miles to go before *we* sleep.

Miles to go before we sleep.

Fifteen

Harper said, "Have you seen Wexford this morning, Nicholas?"

Augustine had been loading a pipe from a humidor of tobacco, but now he paused. "No, I haven't. Why?"

"I stopped by his compartment a little while ago. I wanted to talk to him—"

"Talking to him won't do any good, Maxwell."

Harper repressed an annoyed sigh. "The point is," he said, "Wexford wasn't in his compartment. Nor was he there last night when I first went to talk to him. Nor was I able to find him anywhere else."

Augustine frowned. "That's odd."

"I'd say so, yes."

There was a moment of silence as Augustine put the cold pipe between his teeth, gnawed reflectively on the stem. It was just past seven A.M. and they were sitting in the President's office, where Harper had found him sipping coffee and scribbling what he said were "campaign notes" on a scratch pad. Pale sunlight gave the compartment a dusty, almost elegiac aura. Beyond the windows patterns of early-morning mist drifted among the mountain evergreens like smoke from smoldering fires; the view made Harper feel cold.

His lips curving in a faint smile, Augustine said finally, "Maybe the bastard fell off the train during the night."

Harper stiffened. "That's not at all humorous, Nicholas. We have enough problems without any more of your ill-timed wit."

The words came out more sharply than he had intended, but Augustine seemed to take no offense. He said only, "Yes, I expect you're right," and made sucking sounds on the pipe stem, as if it were lighted and he was trying to get it to draw. "Well then, he's around somewhere. He'll turn up by the time we arrive at The Hollows at nine."

"I can't wait until then," Harper said. "There'll be press people at the station. And you told me yourself you'd disinvited him to join us at the ranch."

"All right. If it will make you happy, ask Christopher to find him for you. Tell him I said to take care of it."

"I'll do that," Harper said. He stood, paused. "If you want to be present when I talk to Julius, I can have Justice bring him here—"

"No," Augustine said. "Definitely not. I don't want to see or listen to that son of a bitch today."

Now he's turned petulant, Harper thought. He said, "Just as you say, Nicholas," in a neutral voice, and went to the door and out into the corridor.

Maybe the bastard fell off the train during the night.

The President's words echoed in his mind as he made his way forward to the security's Pullman. God, suppose something like that *had* happened to Wexford? Ridiculous, of course. And yet, was it really any more ridiculous than some of the other things which had happened of late? When matters degenerated toward chaos, anything was possible. Anything at all.

But Wexford hadn't had an accident, wasn't dead; he was alive and well somewhere in the bowels of this damned mechanical serpent. Of course he was.

Maybe the bastard fell off the train during the night. . . .

Sixteen

At first Justice did not think much about Maxwell Harper's—and the President's—request that he locate the attorney general. It was routine enough: Wexford wasn't immediately available and either Harper or Augustine wanted to talk to him, so someone had to be dispatched to fetch him. And where routine was concerned, you didn't stop to draw conclusions. You just went ahead and did what you were told.

He went first to Wexford's compartment, but the room steward was there making up the berth and told him that he hadn't seen the attorney general since last night. From there he went down to the dining car and spoke with two of the waiters; both of them said Wexford had neither come in for breakfast nor sent for it. Frowning a little then, Justice entered the club car. It was empty, shades drawn against the thin sunlight. He walked through it to the observation car, where Ed Dougherty was sitting alone with the current issue of the *Congressional Record.* When Justice asked him about Wexford, Dougherty shook his head and said that the last he'd seen of him had been after midnight, out on the observation platform, just before he himself had retired. He'd been alone then, having a smoke and taking some air because he couldn't sleep.

Justice stepped out onto the platform and stood for a moment with his hands on the iron railing. Apprehension had begun to grow in him—a fearful suspicion that he did not want to believe. He took several deep breaths of mountain air that was bracingly cold, damp with mist that drifted across the right-of-way and curled sinuously along the surrounding slopes. In the distance the snow-draped shoulders of the Sierra Nevada peaks were visible beneath clouds of sunlit fog; Justice stared at them without really seeing them.

What could have happened to Wexford? he thought.

He returned to the aides' Pullman and spoke with another steward, with Frank Tanaguchi, with Elizabeth Miller. Negative. He went into the security's Pullman and asked two agents if they had seen the attorney general. Negative. He went forward and looked through the train staff's car, the baggage car. Negative. He came back and checked the communal lavatories in the staff car and in each of the Pullmans. Negative.

That left him only one option—to begin knocking on compartment doors. He did that, and each time there was a response he was careful to keep his questions casual so as not to arouse curiosity. At those compartments where no one answered his knock, he opened the door just long enough to make a visual check of the interior. He even glanced into the President's private drawing room, and through the open door of the First Lady's drawing room as a steward delivered a tray of coffee and toast.

Negative.

His stomach was knotted with tension by the time he finished. He stood uncertainly in the swaying corridor of the aides' Pullman, trying to decide what to do next. Inform the

President? No; he had to be absolutely *sure* the attorney general was nowhere on board before he said anything, raised even that much of an alarm. Go over the train again, each of the cars in turn. But no more inquiries—and no alerting the other agents, at least not yet, not until the President was consulted.

He hurried down to the observation car, started there and worked his way forward to the baggage room. His search was careful, thorough. And it yielded nothing.

There could no longer be any doubt: Wexford had vanished from the Presidential Special.

What had happened to him?

Then his mind closed, as if defensively sealing itself off from the question. Through the baggage car window he became aware of a familiar landmark: a large lumber mill, plumes of wood-smoke fanning upward from its chimney stacks, and a series of smaller rustic buildings surrounding it—the village of Greenspur, situated less than ten miles from The Hollows. Justice glanced at his watch, confirmed that it was a quarter of nine. They would reach The Hollows station in less than fifteen minutes.

He left the baggage car and began to hurry through the corridors to U.S. Car Number One.

Seventeen

Augustine was about to leave his office and join Claire when Maxwell returned and asked if Justice had reported back.

"No," Augustine said. "You mean he hasn't turned up Wexford for you yet?"

"Certainly that's what I mean," Harper said. "I've been waiting in my compartment for the last hour. Nicholas, I'm frankly becoming concerned about—"

And there was a sudden sharp, urgent rapping on the office door.

They exchanged a brief look, and immediately Harper went to the door and slid it open. Justice. He seemed to hesitate at the sight of Harper, then came quickly into the compartment and stood uneasily with his arms flat against his sides. Looking at him, at the distressed planes of his face, Augustine thought with cold alarm: My God, there *is* something wrong—

"Mr. President," Justice said, "may I speak to you privately?"

Harper shut the door and came over in front of him. "Is it about Wexford?"

Justice hesitated.

"Is it about Wexford?"

"Yes sir."

"Then for Christ's sake, man, spit it out."

"Mr. President?"

"Yes, yes," Augustine said, "go ahead, Christopher."

Justice took a breath, let it out sibilantly. "I couldn't find him," he said. "I'm sorry, sir, but he's ... disappeared."

A tic began to flutter Augustine's left eyelid. "Disappeared?"

"Yes sir."

"Are you *sure* of that?"

"Positive, sir. I've been through the entire train twice; I looked everywhere."

Harper said, "Jesus."

The same kind of shock Augustine had felt two nights ago in Washington, when Justice brought him the news of Briggs's fatal accident, seemed to take hold of him again. "It isn't possible," he heard himself say. "How could a thing like that *happen?*"

"I don't know, sir," Justice said. "But Mr. Dougherty told me he saw Mr. Wexford out on the observation platform last night, after midnight. Maybe he lost his balance when the train lurched, or had a stroke or something, and ... well, fell off the platform."

Harper pivoted and stared at Augustine as if in accusation. But I was only joking earlier, Augustine thought numbly. I never imagined it might be true. How could I imagine anything like that would be true?

"What should we do, sir?" Justice asked him.

"Do?"

"Yes sir."

Harper said, "There's nothing to do," in a curiously dull,

hollow voice—a tone Augustine had never heard him use before.

"But there's a chance he might still be alive, badly hurt somewhere along the tracks—"

"Don't be a fool, Justice. A man Wexford's age could never survive a plunge from a speeding train."

"I guess you're right, Mr. Harper. Still, shouldn't a search party be sent out right away?"

"Yes," Augustine said. "A search party."

He went behind his desk, sank heavily into the chair. I hated Julius, he thought, I hated him for what he tried to do to me—but he was a friend for twenty years, I never wanted him dead. I never wanted Briggs dead either. Briggs. And now Wexford. One is bad enough, but two; two. No way to cover this one up, even if I wanted to. And Briggs will be found anytime now back in Washington.

Why did they have to die? Goddamn them, why did they have to do this to me?

Outside, the train's air horn echoed loudly through the quiet morning. Augustine lifted his head, realized that the Presidential Special had slackened speed and that they were passing through the long limestone-walled cut into the narrow valley where The Hollows station was located. Less than five minutes now before arrival.

He also realized Justice was speaking to him. " . . . all right, sir?"

"What did you say?"

"I asked if you were all right, Mr. President."

"Yes. A little shell-shocked, that's all."

"Do you want me to have Communications radio in a report to the FBI?"

"No," Harper said.

Justice shifted his gaze. "Sir?"

"What's happened is terrible enough without risking an immediate leak to the media. We can contact the FBI directly from The Hollows; a half-hour or so isn't going to make any difference to Wexford. And there'll be time to prepare an official announcement for when the body is found." He looked at Augustine. "Don't you agree, Mr. President?"

"Yes," Augustine said.

"Then that's how we'll handle it." And to Justice, "Not a word to anyone, do you understand?"

Justice seemed to want to say something; instead he nodded grimly, silently.

Augustine thought: Why couldn't they all have been as strong and as loyal as Maxwell and Christopher? And Claire too ... Claire. God, what will *she* say? I've got to tell her— but not right away, not until we get to The Hollows. I can't face her with it until then.

"We'll be at the station any minute," Harper said. "Can you put up a front for the media, Nicholas?"

Augustine looked across at the liquor cabinet, then immediately pulled his eyes away from it again. "Don't worry about the media," he said.

The air horn sounded another time and the train lost more of its speed, coasting as they neared the station.

Augustine got slowly to his feet. "We've all got things to do before we disembark," he said. "We'd better do them."

Harper nodded. "Just the amenities at the station and straight to The Hollows. All right?"

"Yes. All right."

When they were gone Augustine stood staring at the closed door. How can I beat them now that Wexford is dead too? he thought, and felt a coldness settle on the back of his neck.

How can I beat them now?

Eighteen

Justice finished repacking his suitcase and stood at his compartment door. The Presidential Special had already stopped, and outside the windows, on the station platform, there was a good deal of noise and activity. But he did not pay any attention to it. He might have been alone somewhere, standing in utter silence. He knew the name of the fear now that had been plaguing him since Thursday night, and the voice of it echoed in his mind and would not be shut away.

What if something far more ominous had happened to Briggs and Wexford, the voice kept saying, than death by freak and coincidental accident?

What if they were murdered?

What if someone close to the President was a homicidal psychopath?

PART THREE
The Hollows

One

Harper disembarked from the Presidential Special prior to
Augustine and the First Lady, as was customary for the staff
aides, and walked quickly through the mixed crowd of
media people and security officers on permanent assignment
to The Hollows. He kept his expression carefully blank, but
it felt brittle, like something made of thin opaque glass.
Inside him there was a kind of bitter hopelessness; he did
not let himself dwell on it, kept it under rigid control, but it
was there and he could not rid himself of it.

He stood alone at the far end of the station platform,
segregated from the crowd by the stolid bodies of Secret
Service personnel, and waited and watched his breath puff
whitely on the cold morning air. The glare of sunlight
reflecting off the metal surfaces of the train hurt his eyes and
he wished vaguely that he had adopted the affectation of
sunglasses—dark ones to dull not only the glare but his
perception of the sharp edges of the valley.

Sharp edges. An accurate phrase, he thought with distaste. The pointed tops of pine and spruce and those

overrated California monoliths, the redwoods. The jagged crowns of distant mountain peaks. The sawtooth tips of the valley slopes. The knifelike blades of the rail tracks, the axlike blades of the long limestone cut through which the tracks passed. The thin serrated-looking security fences that stretched away on both sides of the asphalt road beyond the station. The corkscrew line of the road up and across the eastern ridge toward the ranch complex in a second "hollow." Even the station itself—an old wood-and-stone structure that had once been part of a logging railhead in the days before Philip Augustine had built The Hollows—with its alpine roof and its square stone chimneys and its sloping platform ceiling.

He hated this place, The Hollows. He was city-bred and city-oriented, an urbanite in every respect; the so-called great outdoors had always given him an unsettled feeling of inefficacy, as though these sharp open spaces somehow abrogated both his worth and his ability to maintain complete control. A mild form of agoraphobia, he supposed; but there was nothing to be done about it.

He drew the collar of his overcoat tighter around his neck. The morning seemed hushed despite the faint chuffing of the locomotive and the murmur of voices from the crowd. Nothing moved anywhere except here on the platform. On the far slopes thin waterfalls of melting snow, cascading down to the hidden Yurok River which ran through The Hollows, seemed motionless in perspective—white veins in the green tracery of trees. Even those high patches of mist which had not already burned off clung to pines and redwoods like giant gray spiderwebs.

The edge of the world, Harper thought—and Augustine and Claire finally appeared and started down the metal steps from the train.

The crowd stirred to attention. Harper moved closer, saw that Augustine wore his public face like a mummer's mask and that he appeared to be in relatively good command of himself. The stress lines were visible enough, but not so apparent as to alert the reporters. At his side, wearing a black alpaca coat and a stylish cossack hat over her blonde hair, Claire smiled and waved with a kind of detached reserve. Her face was pale and her eyes looked huge and dark. Harper wondered if Augustine had told her yet about Wexford. He wondered what her reaction had been or would be. He wondered again if he would ever know—not that it seemed to matter any longer—what her motivations and her feelings truly were.

As they started across the platform, Augustine saying to the reporters, "No questions right now, ladies and gentlemen, I'm sorry," Harper saw Justice come down the stairs, the last of the Secret Service agents to leave the train. No public face on him, nor any of his usual stoicism; he looked far more troubled and worried than he had in Augustine's office. His eyes, fixed straight ahead, had a remote quality, as if he were not wholly aware of externals.

Augustine led the way swiftly through the station and out to where a phalanx of automobiles—The Hollows' limousine, a pair of sleek Cadillacs, a mixture of security cars and station wagons—waited bumper-to-bumper in a long straight line, like an unintentional parody of the Presidential Special. He helped Claire into the rear of the limousine, slid in beside her without turning to face the reporters again. Framed in profile behind the window glass, his face to Harper had the look of a bust inexpertly chiseled from old gray stone.

Harper went to the second of the Cadillacs because the first had already been claimed by other aides. The reporters and photographers and television crewmen milled around in a frustrated way, radiating a faint aura of hostility at the President's summary treatment of them. One of the reporters started toward Harper, who got quickly into the Cadillac and moved across to the opposite window. Justice followed him inside, as did Ed Dougherty; Elizabeth Miller already sat in the front seat, another Secret Serviceman beside her at the wheel. Outside, the reporter stood grimacing, hands on hips. Harper smiled out at him professionally, thinking: To hell with you, my friend; to hell with all of you.

Even before the other cars in the caravan were loaded, the President's limousine pulled away from the station and onto the asphalt road. Both Cadillacs followed immediately. Harper glanced at Justice beside him: still looking straight ahead, hands flat on his knees. Miller and Dougherty also seemed disinclined to talk, which suited Harper. He tucked a hand under his chin and tried not to look out at the passing scenery.

It was a six-mile drive from the station to the ranch, and for most of that distance the road serpentined—more sharp edges—through dense forest. But near the crest of the ridge which separated the two valleys, the trees thinned out and there was a short stone bridge that spanned a limestone-and-granite gorge. The Yurok River, swollen with snow runoff, raced through the gorge two hundred feet below with such speed that its surface was coated with swirls of white foam. A thousand yards farther on, the road straightened briefly across the flat ridge crown, then began its descent. As they started down, following the first Cadillac and the limousine, the second valley and The Hollows appeared beyond the windshield.

The overview reminded Harper, as on previous visits and unpleasantly, of a huge open-air amphitheater. The valley floor was flat, and on all sides of the ranch complex, rolling green meadowland stretched away to the encircling slopes and ridges. The complex itself sat in the exact center of the valley, ringed widely by a high security fence which government architects had designed so that it blended into rather than detracted from the country-estate landscaping. In the exact center of the complex was the manor house, a huge sprawling single-story structure built of redwood and native stone. Behind it, to the east, was an arrangement of six private guest cottages; on its north side were tennis courts, a covered swimming pool, and a garden patio shaded by black oaks; on its south side were garage barns, accommodations for personal staff and security officers, stables and a paddock and corral for Augustine's complement of horses. Outside the security fence, riding paths wound through the meadow-land in three directions, leading up into various parts of the forest and beyond into the rangeland hills and shallow valleys that comprised the bulk of the thousand-acre ranch. But the only road into or out of the valley below was the one on which they were traveling.

Harper's stomach began to feel queasy as the Cadillac started through a series of sharp, descending curves. I don't want to be here, he thought. I don't want to be trapped in all this goddamn wilderness. All I want—

The car jounced suddenly, skidded for an instant as the Secret Serviceman at the wheel took one of the curves with too much speed and was forced to brake in abrupt compen-sation. The bucking motion pitched Harper into Justice, jarring both of them. Dougherty said something in warning to the driver, who muttered a deferential apology and allowed their speed to decrease and the distance between the two Cadillacs to lengthen.

Harper pushed away from Justice again, leaned against the padded side panel and listened to the sour rumbling in his stomach. His mind seemed to have gone blank, as if the jarring had caused a minor short-circuit in his thought processes. He no longer knew what he wanted, or cared because it seemed evident enough that he was not going to get it.

Not now and not ever.

Two

As we approach The Hollows we are troubled, far more troubled than we were on the Presidential Special because a new insight has come to us. We have executed two traitors, committed two acts of mercy—but how many other traitors are there still to be dealt with? How many more acts of mercy are necessary in order to end the conspiracy against the President? One, two, five, a dozen, a score?

Too many?

Perhaps, in our zeal, we have set ourself an impossible, an ultimately futile task. If there are too many of these turn-coats, how can we continue to execute them with impunity? There can only be so many "accidents" before those who are our enemies, or those who are our friends but who do not understand the need for corporal punishment, realize the truth and take steps to nullify *us*.

And yet, we cannot—we must not—stop now. We are committed, we must go on, we must try to wipe out the conspiracy before it destroys Nicholas Augustine and all that he stands for. We must!

One thing is certain: no matter what happens, others of them will die. Kineen, and the next traitor whose deceit we are positive of—those two, at the very least, *will* die to protect the sanctity and the glory of the President of the United States.

Three

Sitting on the Cadillac's rear seat, Justice kept thinking: *Was* it murder, what happened to Briggs and Wexford? *Is* someone close to the President a psychopathic killer?

He did not want to believe it. Yet years of experience in police work had taught him to distrust extreme coincidence, and you could not find any more extreme coincidence than two fatal accidents to two high-ranking political figures in as many days. And even though his conscious mind had refused to consider it, there had been a small suspicion in him from the beginning, from the moment he had found Briggs's body under the office window, that the press secretary might not have died by accident—the seed that had spawned the lingering fear.

A psychopath. Every person had homicidal tendencies; that was a proven psychological fact. In most people they were buried deeply, and in others they came closer to the surface but were held in careful check; but in some individuals the impulse to murder became too great, eventually controlled reason and exploded into violence. Usually when that happened the person ran amok; in rarer instances he turned cunning and clever and committed his crimes in secret, so that you had no way of telling just by looking at him or talking to him that he was psychotic. Justice had read about such cases, had even investigated one during his time on the Washington police force—a mild-mannered business executive with a wife and three children who had strangled four women in the space of three months before he was finally caught. It could happen, it had happened, to people from all races, creeds, professions, classes, and intellects. And that meant it could happen to someone in the hierarchy of the U.S. government.

But even a psychopath had motives. If someone had murdered Briggs and Wexford—why?

Blank.

Justice did not know what to do. His training demanded that he immediately take his suspicions to the President, or at least to his superiors in the Secret Service. And yet, suppose he was wrong? Suppose he was creating a monster out of misfortune and anxiety? He had no proof, not even a shred of circumstantial evidence; he had nothing but an ugly, half-formed hunch. There was no reason why the President should believe him, no reason why his superiors should believe him. And he could not go to his superiors in any case, he realized, because then he would have to tell them about Briggs, whose body had still not been discovered in Washington. (And why hadn't it been? *Somebody* should have found him by now.) Then the removal of the corpse from the White House might come to light, and that was something he could not take responsibility for. He had given the President his oath of silence.

All right, then. The only other alternative was to find proof himself. But how? In mystery novels the detectives solved all sorts of bizarre and improbable crimes by incisive questioning and astute observation, by stringing together clues to establish a pattern of truth. But he was no deductive genius like Poirot or Peter Wimsey or Gideon Fell; he lacked the capacity for ratiocination. He was nothing more than a simple working police officer, and simple working police officers conducted their investigations on the basis of evidence and fact....

They were almost to The Hollows now. Ahead, through the windshield, Justice could see the President's limousine approaching the main gate to the ranch complex. Then he became aware of Ed Dougherty sitting on his left, Maxwell Harper on his right, Elizabeth Miller in the front seat. One of them? he thought. Or the agent, Judson, at the wheel? One of the other staff aides? One of the other security people? Who?

Who?

The main gate swung open electronically as the limousine neared it, and the caravan proceeded onto the estate grounds. As always, there was an aura of pastoral serenity to the landscaped lawns and outer gardens, the redwood-and-stone buildings, the horses roaming inside the paddock and the split-log corral; but this time it struck Justice as false illusion, like a set for a movie in which terror was the dominant theme.

If murder had been done in the White House and on the Presidential Special, it could be done here too.

Four

When the limousine drew up in front of the manor house, Augustine stepped out immediately and then reached back inside to give his hand to Claire. The two Cadillacs pulled up behind the limousine; the other cars had veered off onto the branch road that led to the garage barns and the staff and security quarters.

With Claire standing beside him, Augustine gazed around the ranch acreage. He tried to tell himself it was good to be home again—but it was not good except in a superficial way. The familiar sights and sounds and smells offered little comfort, little peace. The bastards have taken this away from me too, he thought.

The permanent domestic staff of The Hollows, headed by Walt and Ella Peterson, an elderly couple who had been with the Augustine family for thirty years, came out from the house. Augustine forced himself to feign cheerful responses to their greetings, and when Elizabeth Miller joined them he left her and Claire to answer the Petersons' questions about lunch and other household matters, and walked over to where Maxwell and Christopher and the others were standing.

Justice, he saw, seemed to be in a state of anguish, as if there were conflicts raging inside him. And for the first time since he had known the man, Harper appeared listless, empty of his usual self-assurance. The others wore sober expressions, unaware of all the facts but sensitive to the grim tenor of things.

Faces before the fall? Augustine thought, and tightened his lips to keep from wincing. He said, "The day is yours, gentlemen. We'll table business discussions until tomorrow."

Small frowns of protest. Dougherty said, "But Mr. President ... "

"We can all use a short break," Augustine said. "Besides which, I have personal matters to attend to today and I'd rather not be disturbed."

He turned away from them, to escape their eyes and to shut off further protest, and walked quickly to the house. But as he came up onto the wide roofed porch, Harper hurried up behind him and touched his arm. Augustine stopped, looked at him.

"Nicholas," Harper said in a low voice, "I don't think tabling business matters is a good idea. There are pressing issues to be dealt with as soon as possible—the Indian situation, the S-1 bill, campaign strategy—"

"I can't face those things today."

"You've *got* to face them."

"Tomorrow," Augustine said. "I need time to get my head together. I just can't think about domestic issues of campaign strategy after what happened to Julius."

"Yes," Harper said bitterly, "Julius. You'll notify Saunders at the FBI right away, won't you?"

"Naturally. We settled that on the train."

"Yes. *We* settled it on the train."

"Don't be sarcastic, Maxwell."

Harper gave him a bleak look. "Of course you'll tell

Saunders the search has to be conducted with the utmost secrecy—"

Irritation made Augustine say in louder tones than he'd intended, "Don't tell me how to deal with a security problem, damn it."

In alarm Harper stared at him, then past him, and Augustine realized abruptly that his voice must have carried. He swung around and saw Claire and Elizabeth Miller and the domestic staff looking over at him, Claire with an expression of startled concern. But at least the rest of his aides had already moved off toward the guest house; only Justice still stood by the Cadillacs.

Augustine brought himself under control again, managed to smile at Claire and the others in an apologetic way, and looked back to Harper. "*Mea culpa*, Maxwell," he said wearily. "We'll talk later."

Tight-lipped, Harper nodded. And turned and stalked down off the porch.

Augustine entered the house. All the window curtains were open in the massive beam-ceilinged family room, admitting intersecting funnels of sunlight in which dust motes tumbled against one another like tiny insects. Mica particles glittered in the stone face of the fireplace; the redwood wall paneling and the antique Victorian furniture glistened with wood polish. The effect was one of bright, cheerful elegance that at other times would have given him a warm feeling of complacency, of nostalgia for all the carefree days spent here with his father and with Claire. Now he merely glanced into the room, noted it without thought or emotion, as he would have noted a room in the house of a stranger, and walked away from it toward his study at the rear.

When he reached the study he saw that it too was bright with sunlight, and immediately went to the windows and drew the drapes. Like the family room, and the formal parlor and the library and the conference room and each of the five bedrooms, the study was paneled in redwood. Shelves and glass cabinets lined two of the walls and were stocked with more of his collection of railroadiana: postcards, company rule books, equipment manuals, rate guides, dining-car silver and china, uniform buttons and badges and patches. Against a third wall was a long, wide table on which sat a toy train layout—O-gauge track, miniature station houses, crossing signs and semaphores, working models of Ives and Lionel and Dorfan cars and locomotives from the early 1900s.

Augustine went to his desk, filled a calabash with tobacco, and then crossed to the toy train board and plugged in the electrical cord and threw the switch. Chewing on the curved stem of the pipe, he watched tiny signal lights flash and one of the Lionel locomotives pull a string of freight cars around the network of tracks.

Behind him, then, the study door opened and Claire's voice said, "Nicholas?"

He turned. She came inside, closed the door and walked slowly to where he stood. Her eyes were steady on his face, probing, as they had been when he joined her on the Presidential Special and from time to time during the silent ride out from the station. She knew, of course, as she always seemed to know, that something was wrong. Outwardly she appeared calm and reserved—she would have made a brilliant actress, he thought, not for the first time—but he had been able to feel the tension in her when she held his hand inside the limousine, could almost see it in her as she faced him.

Quietly she said, "Do you want to talk now?"

"Yes. But I wish I could spare you from it."

"Is it that bad?"

"It's that bad."

Her breath made a sibilant sound as she exhaled. "Tell me," she said

He heard the faint chattering of the toy train speeding

around the tracks, abruptly reached back to shut off the switch. The room became silent—an acute silence that seemed charged with a shrillness not quite perceived, like a shriek just beyond the range of human hearing.

"Wexford disappeared from the train last night," he said. "It appears as though he fell off the observation platform."

Claire closed her eyes, seemed to sway for a moment; emotion flickered like shadows across her face. Then she shook herself visibly and regained her poise, and the emotion vanished as though behind a mask that had momentarily slipped. She said, "When did you find out about this?"

"Earlier this morning. Christopher searched the Presidential Special just before we arrived."

"Who else have you told?"

"Just Maxwell. I've got to call Washington and talk to Saunders at the Bureau, have him instigate a search—"

"No," Claire said, "not yet."

"I know what you're thinking. But there's nothing we can do this time, no way we can begin to cover up. Don't you think I've already considered that? The longer we delay, the worse it's going to be when the facts come out."

"The facts," she said woodenly. "First Austin and now Julius. God help us."

"Yes," Augustine said, "God help us."

She hugged herself. "What are we going to do, Nicholas?"

"I don't know," he said. "I've got to think. I need time to think, to make some sort of decision."

Claire was silent for a moment, then she said softly, "You *do* have to make a decision now. You know that, don't you."

"Yes," he said.

To her credit, she did not say anything more about it; they both knew what that decision involved, and she sensed that he needed to reach it alone, without any more discussion. She said only, "Would you like me to call Saunders in Washington?"

"That's my responsibility."

"Let me help you where I can, Nicholas. Please."

"All right," he said because he did not really want to do it himself. "You know what to tell him?"

"I know." Claire came forward, kissed him tenderly on the cheek. Up close, her eyes were shiny and moist—windows, dark windows. "I'll be in the house if you need me," she said.

When he was alone again Augustine pulled a chair over in front of the board and switched the toy train back on and sat down to stare at it. Lights flashed, semaphores waved, signals changed as the miniature rolling stock traveled along the interconnected tracks. Going around and around in intricate loops. Going nowhere at all.

Five

Justice spent the morning in his room at the security quarters—drinking cup after cup of black coffee, pacing the room, sitting in one of the chairs, mechanically unpacking his suitcase after it was delivered by one of The Hollows' staff. But by noon the passive waiting, and the caffeine, had set his nerves to jangling so badly that getting out of there became a matter of self-defense.

He wandered over to the manor house, circled it without seeing any sign of the President. As he walked toward the guest houses it occurred to him to seek out Maxwell Harper; he needed desperately to discuss his suspicions with someone and Harper was a logical choice. But then he thought: What if *he's* the psychopath? It could be him; it could be anyone. Justice shivered faintly in the warm sunlight, veered away toward the patio and the swimming pool. He had never felt more alone in his life.

There was no one by the pool except for a maintenance man cleaning leaves from the water with a long-handled screen. Three gardeners worked among the flowers and shrubs in the surrounding gardens. An almost breathless hush seemed to envelop the ranch, as it almost always did in spring and summer. Even the cries of birds, the drone of insects was muted.

Justice walked past the tennis courts, through the wall of black oaks to the east fence, back along the fence behind the guest cottages. Through the east gate he saw what appeared to be three men on horseback, making their way along the northeast riding trail. He went across to the paddock. Three more horses moved lazily inside the split-log fencing; the smell of their manure was pungent here. He walked around past the stable, looked in through the open double doors and noticed three ranch hands in Western garb working inside.

And came to an abrupt halt. Threes, he thought. Three gardeners, three riders, three horses, three ranch hands. Clusters of three. Things happen in threes.

He was not a superstitious man; he did not believe in omens. And yet he felt a sudden portent, a vivid and overpowering intimation of tragedy and violence. *There's going to be another murder here at The Hollows.* The hairs on his neck prickled; he could feel the staccato throb of his pulse. *And the victim could be anyone too. It could even be ... God, it could even be the President himself.*

Chills capered along Justice's back. He could not keep his suspicions to himself, not any longer; he couldn't take the risk or the responsibility. He *had* to tell the President.

Justice hurried back to the manor house. No one answered his knock on the front door; everybody was apparently either at the back of the house or gone out elsewhere. Maybe the President is in his study, he thought, and came down off the porch and started back along the north wall.

The French doors to the family room were open now, to admit the faint noonday breeze, and when he reached them he heard the voice of the First Lady from inside, carried clearly on the still air. He hesitated, glancing inside, thinking that she might be talking to the President. But she was alone in the room; she stood with her back to the French doors, speaking into the telephone.

" ... stress too strongly how important this is," she was saying. "No, I don't care to go into details on the phone. How soon can you locate him and have him fly out to California?" Pause. "Yes, all right, I understand. Do whatever you can." Pause. "Yes. Good-bye."

She replaced the receiver, turned immediately before Justice could move, and saw him standing outside. She blinked twice in surprise, put a hand to her breast.

Justice said quickly, "I didn't mean to startle you, Mrs. Augustine. I'm sorry."

She looked at him for a long silent moment, then lowered her hand and came across to the French doors. "What are you doing prowling around out here?"

"I wasn't prowling, ma'am."

"Then what were you doing?"

"Looking for the President," he said.

"He's not here. He left fifteen minutes ago—to go riding,' he said."

"Oh, I see."

She gave him a long probing look, and Justice began to fidget under the scrutiny. He felt awkward in her presence, as he always seemed to; she was such an imposing, inscrutable woman that she made him aware of his inadequacies, his inconsequentiality. It was not a conscious domination on her part, but it was a domination nonetheless. He could understand at moments such as this exactly why she was and had been such a powerful motivating force in the President's life.

At length she said,"I suppose you overheard me on the phone."

"Only for a moment, Mrs. Augustine."

"Do you know to whom I was talking?"

"No ma'am."

"Well, I'll tell you. I was talking to the FBI in Washington. Director Saunders isn't available, but I've asked that he be located and requested to join us here as soon as possible."

"Because of the search for the attorney general?"

"Among other reasons."

"Other reasons?"

"They don't concern you, Christopher."

"Yes ma'am." It was plain to Justice that she wanted to terminate the conversation. "I won't bother you any longer, Mrs. Augustine," he said. "I'll see the President later, after he returns."

He pivoted away, walked back to the front of the house. He sensed that she had stepped out through the French doors and was looking after him, but because he was frowning in contemplation he did not glance back. Why had she asked Saunders to come to The Hollows? he was thinking. What were those other reasons she had spoken of?

Did she also suspect that Briggs and Wexford had been murdered?

Six

Harper rode awkwardly at the President's side on the trail which angled across the valley meadowland to the northeast. Unused to horses, he was filled with the panicky intimation that at any moment the aged gelding would break from trot to canter and then into a full gallop, and that he would be pitched off to shatter a hipbone, fracture his skull, even break his back on the hard earth. He was aware of what had happened to jockeys such as Anthony DeSpirito and Jackie Westrope, not to mention the best of them all, Willie Shoemaker, who had been crushed by a highstrung filly and had lost a year of his career to traction and pain. If it could happen to Shoemaker, rider of six thousand winning races, it could happen to the effete Eastern intellectual Maxwell Harper.

He clung nervously to the reins, body tilted forward over the horse's bobbing neck. Fifty yards ahead of them, the two Secret Service agents riding point (Augustine's term, "riding point"; dialogue from a puerile Western movie, for God's sake) were just entering the dense forest on the northeast slope; the other two agents trotted along thirty yards behind them. The giant redwoods and the mountain peaks loomed above, dark against the clear sky, and looking at them, Harper felt his stomach clench in agoraphobic reaction.

He wished that he had not agreed to come out riding with the President. But Augustine had been persuasive, and Harper had not felt strongly enough about it at the time to argue. It was an opportunity to talk to him, at least. Still, how could you discuss grave political matters with any degree of substance when you were jouncing along on the back of a damned horse?

Harper glanced at the President beside him: sitting erect in the saddle on Casey Jones, his big sleek bay, wearing riding boots and a fringed leather jacket and a broad-brimmed cowboy hat. Like LBJ at his Texas ranch, he thought disgustedly. Trying to prove to the end that he has his own natural element, playing the dual role of Rough Rider and country squire as though his administration wasn't in a state of near-shambles. The Teddy Roosevelt syndrome.

As they followed the broad path upslope into the trees, Augustine gave him a faint smile and said, "You ride like a dude, Maxwell. Relax, sit up straight, grip the saddle with your knees."

"I'm doing the best I can. I'm no horseman."

"I'll say not. You really should take lessons from one of the men."

Lessons, Harper thought. We're facing political annihilation and he sits there talking about riding lessons. "Nicholas," he said, "did you call Saunders?"

"Claire took care of it, yes."

"Why didn't you do it yourself?"

"What difference does it make who called him? He's been called, that's all that matters."

"All right. Did you prepare a statement yet?"

"Statement?"

"For the press when Wexford's body is found."

Augustine did not say anything. They were into the woods now and it was cool and dark and quiet; the only sounds were bird calls, the creaking of saddle leather, the faint clopping of the horses' hooves. The path, carpeted here with pine and redwood needles, had begun to hook to the north, still climbing. Eventually, Harper knew, it would come out of the heavy forest growth near the gorge through which the Yurok River ran, and then parallel the rim of the gorge to an area of high ground called Lookout Point. Augustine claimed the view from there was spectacular. Harper thought it was terrifying and found himself dreading the time they would spend there before turning back.

He said, "About that statement, Nicholas."

Augustine sighed. "Yes," he said, "I'm preparing a statement for the press."

"I'd like to read it when you're finished."

"I'd rather you didn't."

"Why not? I think I have a right to be briefed in advance of what you're going to say."

"The statement concerns more than Julius Wexford," the President said. "In fact, unless he's found within the next eighteen hours, it will not concern him at all."

"What kind of double-talk is that?"

"It isn't double-talk, Maxwell."

"No? Then please enlighten me."

"I told you, I'm preparing a statement for the press. I'm going to deliver it tomorrow morning. I've asked Frank Tanaguchi to call a press conference for ten o'clock."

Incredulously Harper said, "Press conference?"

"Yes."

"What *for*, if not about Wexford?"

"You'll find out tomorrow."

"Good Christ, Nicholas—"

"I have my reasons for not wanting to talk about it beforehand," Augustine said, and dug his heels lightly into the bay's sides. Casey Jones broke into an immediate canter, hooves kicking up small puffs of dust and needles—and in instant consort the gelding surged to match its pace. Harper made a small involuntary cry; panic cut at him again as the muscles rippling along the gelding's back caused the saddle to roll sharply beneath him. He threw his arms around its neck, clinging desperately, his buttocks jarring with small painful thuds against the hard leather seat.

Augustine maintained the trot for more than a minute, until the trees thinned and the trail emerged near the rocky shoulder of the gorge. Harper could hear the muted rumble of the river, and in terror imagined the horse stumbling, rearing, flinging him out of the saddle and across the ground and over the edge. But then Augustine reined the bay back to a slow walk, and the gelding immediately responded in kind. Making wheezing, snorting sounds through vented nostrils, it walked up beside Casey Jones again.

Harper straightened in the saddle, his breath coming rapidly, and caught onto the pommel to steady himself. He saw Augustine looking at him with thin amusement, felt his face flame. He resisted the need to rub at his smarting buttocks and recaptured his dignity by fixing the President with an angry glare.

"What are you trying to do to me?" he said. "You know I can't handle a horse when it starts to run."

"That was hardly a run, Maxwell," Augustine said mildly. "Just a brisk uphill trot."

"I could have been killed."

"Oh, nonsense. Even if you'd fallen off you wouldn't have hurt anything except your pride."

The President urged Casey Jones into a faster walk, giving Harper no opportunity to reply. The gelding lifted its head,

still snorting, but this time—to Harper's relief—it did not
follow suit; it lowered its head again, as if to say "The hell
with it," and continued to plod upward. The bay moved out
to a four-length lead, climbing to Lookout Point where the
two point-riding Secret Service agents waited.

The high ground there was flat and grassy, backed by a
sheer granite wall, bordered on its other sides by forest and
the deep river gorge. Across the gorge the wooded slopes fell
away steeply to the northeast, so that you could see a series
of small grassland hollows and ridges stretching for miles to
the base of a broad, almost perpendicular peak. When
Augustine reached Lookout Point he dismounted, dropped
Casey Jones's reins, and walked over near the precipice. One
of the agents called out to him to be careful. He nodded,
waved at the man in a dismissive way; then he stood with
his hands clasped at his back, staring out at the distant
valleys.

The gelding struggled up the last few yards to the high
ground and stopped without Harper having to draw rein
and immediately began to graze. He dismounted with
awkward care, aware of the eyes of the agents, and flexed his
cramped legs and hips. The air up here was thin; it made
him feel vaguely light-headed as he crossed toward Augustine in hesitant strides.

He stopped five feet short of where the President stood
because the jagged walls of the gorge were visible and his
perspective of the sheer drop to where the river raged
below—more than two hundred feet—made his stomach
churn sourly. Looking at the view to the northeast was no
better; he focused his attention on Augustine and kept it
there.

The President glanced around at him. "Magnificent sight,
isn't it."

"If you say so."

"Like one of those rare dreams," Augustine said, "where

everything is beauty and peace." His eyes were bright, as distant as the valleys. "The Hollows has always seemed that way to me, you know."

Harper said, "Nicholas—"

"When my father was alive, we had two thousand head of cattle out there. Did I ever tell you that, Maxwell? Two thousand head of the finest Herefords and Aberdeen Angus in the world. The Hollows was a working ranch in those days. But it got to be too expensive to maintain the herd, and when we lost a couple hundred head during a disastrous winter I decided to sell it off. It's odd, but looking out there I can almost see the ghosts of those lost cattle—red-and-white and black ghosts grazing in the valleys."

God, Harper thought. He said, "Why did you call a press conference for tomorrow morning?"

"What?"

"I said, why did you call a press conference?"

Augustine released an audible breath. The brightness in his eyes seemed to dull, and he blinked. "And I told you," he said, "I don't want to talk about it."

"I'm entitled to know."

"Are you? I think not."

"Does it have something to do with Israel? With Oberdorfer? With domestic issues? With your campaign?"

"It has something to do with everything," Augustine said. There was a sudden sharpness in his voice. "Now that's all I'm going to say. I'm the President, Maxwell; I'll thank you to remember that." And he turned back to the gorge and his view of the valleys and the ghosts of his vanished cattle.

Harper realized his hands were clenched, flattened them out again. When he pivoted himself he saw the Secret Service bodyguards, all four of them present now, staring over at him and at the President with blank Justice-like faces. He ignored them, walked stiff-backed to where a fallen log formed a bench at the far end of the clearing. He sat on the log and tried not to look at Augustine standing at the rim of the gorge. And kept looking at him in spite of himself.

Press conference, he thought.

Secrecy, he thought.

Christ!

Seven

Yes, Elizabeth, what is it?

You asked me to come by at three o'clock, Mrs. Augustine. Don't you remember?

Three o'clock. Yes.

Is everything all right?

Why shouldn't everything be all right?

Well—you seem preoccupied . . .

Do I? It's because painful decisions have been made in this house today, Elizabeth. Terribly painful decisions.

What decisions?

And they should have been made long before this. Now I pray to God it's not too late.

I don't understand—

You're not supposed to understand.

Mrs. Augustine . . .

No. I've said too much already; I'm talking too much. I suppose it's because you inspire confidence. You always have.

Are you sure you don't want to discuss it?

I can't discuss it. Don't press me, Elizabeth. Please.

All right, Mrs. Augustine.

You'll find out soon enough—part of it, anyway. Everyone will find out soon enough.

Eight

At dusk Saturday night, after a quiet and somewhat mechanical dinner with Claire, Augustine sat out on one of the iron-filigree patio chairs, worrying the bit of a billiard briar and waiting for Justice.

When he and Harper and the bodyguards had returned from their ride at four-thirty, Christopher had approached him outside the stable, looking worried, and asked to speak with him. But he himself had been abstracted and weary of Maxwell's querulous complaints and questions, and he had only wanted to get away quickly to the manor house for a shower and a drink. So he had told Justice he would see him here tonight and then left him there with Maxwell.

He would keep this meeting as brief as possible, Augustine thought. Because it seemed obvious to him what was on Justice's mind, and discussing it endlessly served no constructive purpose. He had already concluded what must be done, while sitting in his study this morning and watching the toy train board, and he was not about to invite painful dialogue by confiding what it was to anyone. Not Justice, not Harper, not any of his other aides. Not even Claire (although he knew she intuited exactly what his decision was). They would all find out at the press conference tomorrow.

Augustine leaned back in the chair and watched a faint breeze ripple the water in the swimming pool. This was the best time of night in the mountains, he thought. Quiet except for the steady fiddling hum of crickets, the air clean and sharp and piney, the sky just turning a glossy purple-black, the pale face of a full moon hanging above the tops of the trees on the western ridge. But it wasn't the same as it once was; there was something missing, something lost and irreplaceable. As there was with trains. Trains still ran across the country, you still saw them, you could still ride on them, but the spirit of railroading had been taken away ...

Justice appeared then, walking rapidly through the garden on the far side of the patio. Augustine watched him come up onto the flagstones and cross past the diving board. There was the same nervous anxiety in his face and in his manner that Augustine had noticed peripherally at the stable earlier.

"Good evening, Mr. President," he said.

"Christopher. Sit down if you like."

"Thank you, sir." Justice took another patio chair to Augustine's left and placed his hands on his knees.

Augustine said, "Am I correct in assuming you want to talk about Briggs and the attorney general?"

"Yes sir."

"Well, before you ask, there has been no word as yet on either of them. I don't understand why Briggs, at least, hasn't been found by now—unless he had made prior arrangements to take yesterday off and to go away for the weekend. That would explain it. In any case, taking everything into account, the fact that he has not been found is best for all concerned."

Justice nodded.

"Did Mr. Harper tell you I've called a press conference for tomorrow morning?"

"No sir. Press conference?"

"Yes. And please don't ask me why or what statement I intend to make."

"Just as you say, Mr. President." With reluctance.

Augustine softened his voice. "I dislike being brusque with you, Christopher. I don't have to tell you that I appreciate all you've done for me, and your concern, and your support; I think you know how grateful I am. It's just that this is a very difficult time and I don't feel in the least comradely."

"I understand, sir."

"Good. Now then—do you have anything specific to discuss? If not, I—"

"There is something specific, yes sir."

"What is it?"

Justice moved uneasily in his chair; night shadows gave his face a brooding cast. "I don't know how to say it, sir. It's . . . well, it's incredible."

"Incredible?"

"Mr. President," Justice said, and stopped, and then blurted, "Mr. President, I think Mr. Briggs and Mr. Wexford may have been murdered."

"*What?*"

"I'm sorry, sir, I think they were deliberately and cold-bloodedly killed by someone who wanted us to believe their deaths were accidents, someone with an unstable mind—"

Astonishment and utter disbelief. Augustine came convulsively to his feet, stood over Justice. "A homicidal maniac? For God's sake, are you trying to tell me there's a homicidal maniac among the people on my staff?"

"That's what I suspect, sir."

"It's monstrous!"

Miserably Justice nodded.

"What proof do you have?"

"None, sir."

"None? You mean you have no evidence at all?"

"No sir. It's just a feeling, an intuition—"

"Christ Almighty, Christopher!"

"Two men have died in two days, Mr. President," Justice said, "that's just too much coincidence; I've been a policeman a long time and I've learned to trust my instincts—"

"Instincts!" The astonishment was gone now; only the unbelief remained. "Do these instincts tell you who it could be?"

"No sir."

"Or why even a lunatic would murder two men?"

Justice shook his head. "I could be wrong, sir, I know that. But I don't think I am. And I'm afraid something might happen here at The Hollows, that someone else's life may be in danger."

"Whose life?"

"I don't know. But ... it could even be yours, sir."

Augustine stared down at him. He had always considered Justice to be the prototype police officer: cool, disciplined, precise to a fault, incapable of wild or unreasonable speculation. But it seemed the strain of the past few days had affected him much more severely than could have been imagined; had filled him with irrational paranoid fantasies. Two murders made to look like accidents, one of the people Augustine had worked closely with for three and a half years a deranged psychopath—preposterous! A potential third murder, another person's life in jeopardy, his *own* life in jeopardy—unthinkable!

He sat down carefully and said to Justice, "Have you told anyone else about this?"

"No sir."

"I see. Well you'd best not. I'll handle it."

Justice's eyes were imploring. "You do believe me, don't you, Mr. President? About the potential danger, I mean."

"I believe that you believe."

"What should we do?"

"What do you suggest we do?"

"Tighten security, first of all. Beyond that ... I'm not sure, sir."

"I'll know," Augustine said gently. "After I've given it some thought I'll know just what to do."

"We don't have much time, sir. I'm sure of that."

Augustine looked away. So am I, Christopher, he thought. We don't have much time left at all.

Nine

The conference room, adjacent to the President's study in the manor house, was a large, oblong enclosure with a stone fireplace at one end. On Sunday morning a podium was set at the other end, and in place of the broad circular conference table which normally sat in the center of the room were several centered rows of folding chairs for the press. Another row of chairs reserved for the staff was arranged along the west side wall, facing the press rows.

Justice sat near the far end of the staff row and looked at the thirty or more reporters who crowded the room. Most of them were from the wire services, the television networks, and California's large daily newspapers; they stood or sat now in small groups, talking among themselves, waiting as Justice was—it was just ten o'clock—for the announcement that the President was ready to begin.

Their voices were muted and interrogative, creating a low rumble of noise that seemed to reverberate off the redwood walls and the high, beamed ceiling. Justice knew they were asking each other the same questions he had asked himself during the night. Why had the President called this press conference, the first at The Hollows in nearly two years? Was he going to make general statements of no particular news interest, or was he going to drop some sort of bombshell?

He turned his head, glanced over at the study door; it remained closed. Three seats to his left, Maxwell Harper was also looking at the door, looking at it and rubbing his hands back and forth along his trouser legs. There was an air of nervous expectancy about him that Justice had never seen before.

Justice's face was damp under the hot room lights; he used the sleeve of his jacket to wipe it dry, to dislodge grains of mucus that clung to his eye corners. Tension and lack of sleep had made him logy. He had spent most of last night patrolling the grounds, maintaining a personal vigil that yielded nothing out of the ordinary—and worrying, worrying, because it had become obvious as time passed and there was no tightening of security that the President had not believed him after all.

Augustine had only been patronizing him on the patio, not in an unkind way but patronizing him nonetheless, as if he thought Justice were suffering from hallucinations. Justice could understand his skepticism—without substantiating proof he might have been skeptical himself if their roles had been reversed—but the fact remained that nothing was being done. The responsibility for the safety of the President and those close to him still rested solely on his shoulders.

He had considered going to the First Lady, telling her of his fears as he had told the President. But if she didn't share those suspicions, if he had misread her motives in calling Director Saunders here to The Hollows, he would only succeed in alarming and even alienating her. Still, he desperately needed an ally, and if there was one person who could persuade the President to take action, it was Mrs. Augustine. Maybe—

The study door opened in that moment and Frank Tanaguchi stepped through and over to the podium. The babble of voices subsided instantly. "If you'll all take your places, please," Tanaguchi said, "the President is about ready to begin."

Those reporters still standing took chairs. When they were all seated, Tanaguchi returned to the study for half a minute, then came out a second time and claimed a chair for himself. The room was completely silent now—an anticipatory, almost eager hush.

It was another sixty seconds before the President appeared; the First Lady was at his side. He wore a suit and tie, as he seldom did at The Hollows, and carried a small sheaf of notes. To Justice, his presence seemed a commanding one; but when he put the notes down on the podium and gripped its edges, his hands might have been trembling a little. Mrs. Augustine stepped behind him to his right, and although there was a chair behind her she did not sit down. She folded her hands at her waist and her eyes did not once leave the President. Her expression was unreadable.

Augustine cleared his throat. "Thank you all for coming, ladies and gentlemen," he said in clear, strong tones. "I won't keep you long because the statement I have to make is brief and I will take no questions at this time. When I return to Washington later this week I will call a major press conference at which I will respond to all questions pertaining to the statement I am about to make, and to other matters as well. Please bear with me on this."

As a body the reporters seemed to lean forward.

The President cleared his throat again. "It is my belief," he said then, "that I have been a good President, that in some ways I have taken the office beyond politics and instilled in it a frank humanism generally lacking in previous administrations. It seems, however, that many of you and many of your colleagues, as well as the opposition party, certain members of my own party, and a large segment of the country-at-large do not concur with these personal beliefs. So be it. I make no apologies, I offer no excuses for anything I have done or said during my term in office. But neither do I wish to endure the continued disfavor of the evident majority of my fellow Americans; neither do I wish to foment divisiveness by pursuing at length the paths of endeavor which my heart and my love for this nation have told me were the right ones."

Surprise and excitement rippled through the crowd. Justice's chest felt tight, as if a hand had bunched all the muscles there into a ligature. He was aware of Harper sitting on the edge of his chair, hands fisted whitely on his knees; aware of the tense expressions on the faces of the other aides. Behind the President, the First Lady still stood immobile and emotionless.

Augustine raised his eyes from his notes, and as if reciting from painful memory he said, "That being the case, ladies and gentlemen, after long and prayerful consideration I have decided to withdraw my name as a candidate for reelection to the presidency. Under no circumstances will I seek or accept my party's nomination at the forthcoming convention in Saint Louis. I intend during the final seven months of my administration to devote all my time and all my energies to the execution of the duties of my office, with particular reference to domestic affairs . . ."

There was more, but Justice did not hear it. A sense of numbness had come over him; he seemed to be hearing the President's voice as if from a great height or distance. He saw the reporters moving in their seats like people straining against invisible bonds, ready to surge upright as soon as they were released. He saw Mrs. Augustine close her eyes, open them again—her only movement, her only reaction. He saw Harper sitting in such a rigid posture that he might have undergone some sort of seizure. He saw the President finish speaking and stack his notes neatly in front of him, looking both melancholy and relieved, like a minister who has just delivered a poignant eulogy.

He saw all of these people, all of these things, without really seeing them, and he thought: No. Just that one word. *No.*

The President gathered up his notes and started to turn from the podium. One of the reporters, unable to restrain himself, called out, "Mr. President, you can't just deliver a statement as momentous as that without—"

"No questions at this time," Augustine said firmly. "I made that quite clear." And with the First Lady at his side, he walked out quickly through the study door.

As soon as he was gone the room came alive with swarming movement. Everyone was on his feet: Harper and Dougherty and Tanaguchi and the other aides hurrying to the study door to escape the reporters, some of the press milling around and others rushing for the outside exit. But Justice only sat immobile in his chair, listening to their voices pound against his ears, the words indistinguishable but the sense of them reaching him clearly.

"He did it by God never thought he'd actually do it the pressure finally got to him it finally wore him down never thought he'd do it . . ."

Ten

Augustine went straight through the study to the hall door, saying to Claire, "I don't want to talk to any of the staff. Tell them I'll call a meeting later today or tomorrow."

"Yes, Nicholas," she said. "Where will you be?"

"In our bedroom."

She nodded, looked at him for a moment with eyes that told him nothing of what she was thinking, what she was feeling. Then, as the conference room door opened to admit a wave of noise and the first of his aides, she turned and started over to it. Augustine hurried out into the hall and shut that door sharply behind him.

When he came into the master bedroom, the mirror over Claire's dressing table gave him an immediate and un-wanted image of himself. Face composed, carriage erect, hands steady now. But his eyes made a lie of the calm exterior; unlike Claire's, they were naked—they revealed exactly what he was feeling, they told the absolute truth.

He put his back to the mirror, took off his jacket and tie and opened the collar of his shirt. Then he went into the

bathroom and washed his face in cold water, patted it dry
with a towel. In the bedroom again he sat on the rough
Indian blanket that covered the big brass bed, to wait for
Claire.

And sitting there he thought: Did I handle it wrong?
Should I have waited until we were back in Washington?
Should I have taken questions out there? No—I did it the
only way I could. It's the hardest thing I ever had to do in
my life, but I did it and it's finished.

Finished.

There was a dampness in his eyes now and he felt like
weeping. But he did not, would not. Any more than he had
been able to go all the way and resign, give in to the
goddamn National Committee and turn the country over to
Conroy for the next seven months. He had been a decent
President, he had done nothing to be ashamed of; resignation was shame, tears were shame—admissions of guilt or
folly or weakness.

They had taken everything else from him but he would
not let the bastards have his soul.

Eleven

We cannot believe it. We are confused, stunned by what we have just heard the President say to the assembled reporters—so confused and so stunned that we feel our very concealment from me, the singular self, to be threatened. The conspirators have won; there are too many of them, their combined efforts were too great for us alone to overcome. They have insidiously drained Nicholas Augustine's will to fight, they have brought him down, they have beaten him into submission. He is lost and we are lost with him.

Or is he?

Or are we?

What if it is not too late, even now, to save him? The rest of the plotters *could* still be exterminated, the conspiracy *could* still be crushed. And the President would then be free to rescind his manipulated decision to withdraw; he is not bound by it, after all, not yet.

Yes. Yes! We must not abandon hope, nor abandon our mission. We must be strong. We must rip the tendrils of

pain and confusion and defeat—weapons of the conspirators—from our mind, cement the fusion of our purpose. It is
not too late.

We are not sure of how many other conspirators there are,
or of their identities. But we have suspicions about at least
one, and those suspicions are enough. No time now for
gathering more evidence; time now only to act, time now
only for the giving of mercy to the besieged President. Act
and mercy. Act of mercy.

Today, tonight, before this day is done, a third traitor
must die.

Twelve

As soon as the President left the conference room, Harper pushed his way through the milling reporters and went straight out to the garage barns and commandeered one of the Cadillacs. Everything about The Hollows had become unbearable now; unless he got away from there, if only for a little while, it seemed as though he would suffocate.

He drove through the main gate and along the access road at a steady fifty miles an hour. There was an impulse in him to drive faster, drive recklessly, but it was checked by his innate caution and by the looming presence of trees and mountains. Two cars jammed with press people passed him; he paid no attention to them, kept his eyes locked on the roadway.

Inside him there was a cold gray void: no bitterness, no resentment, no anger, nothing at all. He had known on an intellectual level since yesterday morning that the end was near, but it was like knowing you had a terminal illness. You weren't dead *yet* and as long as you were alive there was that tiny spark of hope for a miraculous recovery. But now,

now it was over; the end had come at last. Just like that, with one incredible, pathetic statement delivered by an insipid old fool. Career, future, everything meaningful—dead.

Harper took the Cadillac across the western ridge, down into the first valley past the station and the railroad tracks and the Presidential Special like a waiting funeral train, onto a blacktopped country road and finally into the village of Greenspur. After that there were other country roads, a four-lane state highway that followed the course of the Yurok River, still another county road, a string of lumber mills, two more villages. And always the oppressive wilderness of trees and mountains and valleys, green and brown, green and brown, shadowed and shining in the warm May sunlight. . . .

It became as unbearable after a while as The Hollows. What now? he thought dully. Drive all the way to Washington? Ridiculous. Drive several hundred miles to San Francisco and then take a commercial airline to the Capital? Repellent. There was nothing for him in Washington anyway, not now; there was nothing anywhere. But he did not want to go back to The Hollows either. He did not want to see Augustine, or talk to him, or see and talk to anybody else—

Except Claire?

No. Especially not her. Why should he want to see her?

But the thought stayed with him, and because he was tired of driving and sick of the open countryside, because he had to go somewhere and he had no place to go, he turned the car around finally and started back. Got lost twice, but did not stop to ask directions. Found his way to The Hollows by trial and error, by instinct—he didn't need anyone, he would never trust anyone again.

It was almost five o'clock when he reached the front gate and was admitted to the ranch complex. He drove to the garage barns, left the Cadillac there, and without conscious choice found himself walking straight across toward the main house. I don't want to see her, he thought—and came around a curve in one of the south-garden paths and saw her.

He stopped instantly. Unaware of him, she was bending over a bed of flowers, clipping a bouquet of yellow-and-purple lilies with a pair of shears. She wore a blue bandanna around her hair, and gardening clothes, and there was a smudge of dirt on one cheek. Beautiful, Harper thought. His hands were moist. She's the most beautiful woman in the world.

"Mrs. Augustine," he said. "Claire."

She came erect in a jerky motion, shaded her eyes against the sunglare. "What is it, Maxwell?" Cold voice, distant, always so distant and unknowable.

"Where is the President?" he asked.

"Resting."

"Yes, of course. After what he did this morning he needs all the rest he can get."

She moistened her lips: little pink tongue glistening, flicking sensually at soft pink lips. "He did what had to be done," she said.

"Did he?"

"You know he did."

"I don't know anything," Harper said. "But I can see how delighted you are. If it had been up to you, you'd have had him resign, wouldn't you."

"Yes," she said.

"Why? What motivates you?"

"Nicholas motivates me."

"That's all? Just Nicholas?"

Uneasiness had crept into her eyes. "Why are you talking to me like this, Maxwell? What's the matter with you?"

"Nothing is the matter with me," he said, and thought: Why *am* I talking like this? I don't have any right to say these things. Control, control—but that was gone too and he did not seem to care. And the words kept coming out of him, out of the gray void. "I just want to know you, Claire. I want to know what you're really like inside that beautiful head of yours."

"I think I'd better go—"

"No," he said. "Not just yet. Why won't you open yourself up to me? Why are you afraid of me? Is it because you find me hateful and repulsive?"

She shook her head, shook it again, and began to back away from him.

"Or is it because I'm an intellectual and you think I'm incapable of understanding, that I'm just a political machine with no human feelings?"

"I never thought of you as a machine—"

"I think you did," Harper said. "I think that's exactly how you and Nicholas and everyone else have always felt about me. But you're wrong, all of you. I have deeper feelings than any of you ever imagined."

She kept backing away, seemed about to turn and flee—and compulsively he moved toward her, caught her wrists in his hands. The touch of her skin, the silky warmth of it, made him catch his breath, sent little tremors through him. He had not touched her in a long time, had never touched her except for impersonal handclasps; he had never been this close to her, had never had the scent of her heady in his nostrils, had never looked into the depths of her eyes.

"Please," she said, and ducked her face away from him. "Please, Maxwell, let me go."

"I don't want to let you go," he said. Words still coming out of the void, and he could not stop them, did not want to stop them. "I've always wanted to touch you, Claire."

Her eyes on him again, flashing messages that he could not read. "Don't. Don't—"

"I'm a person after all, you see that now, don't you? I'm capable of normal desires, I'm capable of love."

"Please," she said again.

And he heard himself say, "I've been in love with you for a long time, Claire."

She made a sound in her throat, wrenched out of his grasp, and ran through the garden to the house.

Harper just stood there. Feeling empty, feeling awed at himself and what had been hidden away inside him all these years. Thinking: I shouldn't have done it, I shouldn't have done it—but Nicholas shouldn't have done it either.

Thirteen

At nightfall, beneath another full moon and a sky heavy with stars, Justice prowled here and there, back and forth—and a voice in his mind kept repeating: If it's going to happen it will happen tonight; the killer will go after his third victim in the next few hours.

He could not get rid of the feeling. Every nerve in his body was sensitive with it. But where would it happen? Who was the intended target this time? Could it actually *be* the President, for some reason connected to his stunningly tragic withdrawal statement this morning? Justice had no intuitive answers; there was no way he could begin to fathom the workings of a deranged mind. He felt only that someone else was scheduled to die. Tonight.

Tonight.

And he could not be everywhere at once. He was only one man, one man alone. He wanted desperately to spend the night inside the manor house, at the President's side; to talk to him again, try to make him accept the danger. But when he had gone there just before dusk, the housekeeper, Mrs. Peterson, had told him the President was not seeing anyone and had adamantly refused to carry a message to him. On impulse Justice had asked for an audience with the First Lady, and had been told that she was not seeing anyone either.

There had been nothing for him to do then except either to barge into the house—which might have angered and upset the President enough to make him not only refuse to listen but to have Justice confined to quarters—or to go on patrol. So he had gone on patrol, concentrating his vigil on the manor house, the guest cottages, the security and staff quarters. Whenever he encountered another agent on duty, or any of The Hollows' private security police, he stopped and suggested carefully that they be extra watchful tonight; the President's bombshell at the press conference might bring out part of the lunatic fringe, he said, you never knew how people would react to news like that. That was as far as he could go, and it did nothing at all to ease the fear and tension inside him.

He moved now through the gardens behind the manor house. The lights in the President's study were on, he saw, and the idea came to him to hail Augustine from outside, get in to talk to him that way. Justice crossed to the window, stood close to it and then called out, "Mr. President? It's Christopher Justice, sir. I'd like to speak with you."

No response.

"Mr. President?"

No response.

Justice listened. There was a faint electric whirring from within: Augustine's toy train outfit. So the President *was* inside; at least he knew that much. Amusing himself with his toy trains and not responding even out of curiosity to summonses from outside.

Just stay there, sir, Justice thought. Don't leave the house or respond to any other summonses.

Grimly, he turned away.

Fourteen

Inside the study Augustine sat in front of the train board and stared at a 1927 Ives locomotive dragging a string of tankers and coal gondolas around the tracks. I should have gone into railroading instead of politics, he thought. I should have become a highballing engineer on the last of the steam locomotives on the Southern Pacific or the AT&SF. The smell of cinders and burning coal and hot cylinder oil; the pound of the 2-10-4s and the 4-6-2s and 2-8-0s; the round-houses and the freight yards, the high mountain runs and the desert crossings, the close-knit fraternity of railroaders. To hell with trying to shape the destiny of the world. To hell with the thankless futile eviscerating world of politics. Give me anonymity and freedom and dignity. Give me a little joy.

The toy locomotive was just entering the tunnel cut into a green-painted "mountain" on the left side of the board. Augustine reached out a hand, ran fingertips over the rough papier-mâché surface—and the throbbing melody of "John Henry" began to play again inside his head.

John Henry was hammerin' on the mountain
And his hammer it was strikin' fire;
He drove so hard till he broke his poor heart,
And he laid down his hammer and he died,
Lawd, Lawd, he laid down his hammer and he died.

Well they took John Henry to the graveyard,
And they buried him in the sand,
And ev'ry locomotive that comes roarin' by,
Says, "There lies a steel-drivin' man,
Lawd, Lawd," says, "There lies a steel-drivin' man."

Outside the window a voice called out abruptly, "Mr. President? It's Christopher Justice, sir. I'd like to speak with you."

Augustine raised his head and looked over at the drawn curtains. But he did not say anything; he had no desire to talk to Justice tonight. More nonsense about a homicidal maniac, probably. He had enough things preying on his mind as it was, not the least of which was Maxwell Harper.

"Mr. President?"

No, the only person he wanted to talk to was Claire, and he had been putting it off since five o'clock. But what was the point in continuing to put it off? He would have to discuss it with her sooner or later; he might as well get it over with. She was innocent of any wrongdoing, after all; there was no doubt of that. How could there be any doubt of that?

Augustine got to his feet and went out of the study without bothering to shut off the train board. Most of the lights were on, but the house was quiet except for the faint creeks and groans of settling timbers. Almost like the White House, he thought. Almost as if there were ghosts here too—the ghosts of his father and all the years of his life, whispering to him unintelligibly in the night.

Claire was not in the master bedroom, not in the library or the parlor. He heard crackling noises in the family room, and when he entered he saw her bending before the hearth, feeding pine logs heavy with pitch into a blazing fire.

She straightened around as she heard the sound of his footsteps, the orange firelight dancing on her face. She had changed clothes since he'd last seen her: wearing a blue sheath dress now, blonde hair combed out and brushed into waves that clung to her shoulders. When he came up to her he saw that her eyes were solemn—and the illusion that he could plunge into them, become absorbed by them, came over him again. But it was neither an uneasy sensation nor a sexual one this time; it was one of longing, because in absorption there would be escape.

He said, "That's a nice fire," but he was only making words.

A wan smile. "Yes. Are you hungry, Nicholas? I can have Mrs. Peterson fix you something—"

"No," Augustine said. He had skipped dinner because he had no appetite and because he hadn't wanted to talk to her; he still had no appetite, the thought of food made him ill. "I want to ask you something, Claire."

"All right."

He took a breath. "I saw you with Maxwell this afternoon," he said. "The two of you in the south garden."

Her face paled. "You ... saw us?" in a whisper.

"Yes. I came out for a little air and I saw him touching you, I saw you run away from him. I want to know what happened out there."

Moistness glistened in her eyes. Tears? She didn't speak.

"Tell me what happened, Claire. Why was he touching you? What did he say to you?"

"He said ... Nicholas, I don't want to—"

"Tell me!"

"He said he had deeper feelings than any of us imagined,

that he was a human being and not a machine." Her throat worked. "He acted ... strange, different; it frightened me and I ran."

Dully Augustine said, "There's more to it than that."

"No ..."

"Yes. Yes there is. He said something else, didn't he."

"All right. All right. He said he ... he said he was in love with me."

Augustine flinched. Betrayal—again and again and again. Even Maxwell Harper, of all people. Even him. But there was no anger in him; he was beyond the capacity for any emotion as intense as rage. "I see," he said. "Was that the first time he told you how he felt?"

"Yes."

"You had no idea of it before today?"

"I can't lie to you. I ... suspected."

"Why didn't you tell me?"

"There was no point in it. Nothing ever happened."

Nothing ever happened, Augustine thought. "Is that why you've been reluctant to talk about him lately?"

She nodded. "Nicholas, what are you going to do?"

"Do?"

"About Maxwell. About the incident in the garden."

"I don't know yet," he said.

Claire said abruptly, "Fire him."

"What?"

"Fire him. Get him away from here right now, tonight."

He was silent for a time; then he said, "You're sure that's what you want?"

"I'm not sure of anything anymore. Nicholas, I—"

She broke off again. And reached up, touched his cheek with the tips of her fingers. And then almost convulsively pushed past him and hurried across the room.

Augustine stood looking after her, watching her hips move under the blue dress, the blue dress—

John Henry had a little woman,
And the dress she wore it was blue;
She went walkin' down the track and never looked back,
Said, "John Henry I've been true to you,
Lawd, Lawd, John Henry I've been true to you."

Fifteen

Moonshine.

The night is radiant with it as we make our way through the gardens. It paints the darkness with luminous yellows and golds, it softens the shadows and gives them a velvet gloss, it creates an almost religious aura of beauty and peace. It touches us, bathes us with its brilliance, and yet it does not reach us at all. Beauty and peace are strangers to us now. We knew them once, but no more—no more.

There is no moonshine in our soul; there is only warm black.

When we near the southernmost guest cottage we see that there are lights showing faintly behind drawn front-window shades. But of course we have expected to find him awake; it is only a few minutes past eight o'clock. Is he alone? We will have to take the chance that he is, and return later if he is not.

We walk through the moonshine to the door, putting our hand in our coat pocket to conceal the bulge of the heavy glass ashtray we have placed there. A moment after we knock the door opens, and he peers out at us with listless eyes: the cool Harvard intellectual is gone and in his place stands a derelict. Is it because his sins weigh heavily on his mind? No matter. Treason is treason; remorse means nothing.

"What do you want?" Harper says in a wooden voice.

Behind him we can see most of the room, and it is empty. "We ... that is, I'd like to talk to you," we say.

"Talk about what?"

"May I come in?"

It is obvious that he does not want to be alone with us, and just as obvious that he does not care enough to refuse. He shrugs finally and says, "I suppose so, if you make it brief."

"Oh I will. Very brief."

He steps aside, and we enter past him and walk three careful paces into the room. We turn as he closes the door. He stands with his back to it and hides his hands inside the slash pockets of the dressing gown he wears. The dressing gown is rust-hued, the color of dried blood. We wet our lips; the ashtray is warm against our palm.

Harper says, "Well? What is it you came to say?"

We move over in front of him, close enough so that we can smell the faint sour odor of his breath. He avoids our eyes. "Just good-bye," we say. "Good-bye, Maxwell."

And we bring the ashtray out of our coat and club him with it across the bridge of the nose.

But it is a glancing blow, a sharp corner penetrates the skin and brings a spurt of blood, we have attacked with too much haste this time—and he screams. The others did not scream but Harper shrieks in a thin shrill voice, like a woman, and the sound of it—God, the awful sound of it!—fills us with a kind of wild desperate confusion. We hit him again as he staggers, but his hands are clapped to his forehead, blood streaming over the hands, and the ashtray strikes only his knuckles and he screams again, reels off a table and falls to his knees, screaming, still screaming. We know we have to shut off that sound before someone is alerted, before the pitch of it shatters our brain like crystal, and we rush forward and drive the ashtray against the back of his head, drive him flat to the floor, fall beside him and hit him again and then it stops, at last it stops, and he is still and silent and we know he is dead.

The confusion still has control of us; our head has begun to ache intolerably. We're afraid, for the first time we're terrified.

And inside us something seems to be happening—

We stand again, panting, and stare down at Harper. The back of his skull is crushed and bloody. We can't make this one look like an accident, they'll know it's murder. But there is nothing we can do now, and—

—we're losing the fusion, that's what is happening inside us, *we're* losing control—

Still holding the ashtray. When we look at it we see our fingers smeared with crimson, Harper's blood on our hand. We fling the ashtray away from us, hear it bounce and clatter across the floor, then frantically scrub my fingers—

—*our* fingers, scrub our fingers clean on the tail of his dressing gown. Then I back away

We back away, we do it. But I is trying to take over and we mustn't let me do it. Get out of here before I realizes the truth! We turn blindly and stumble to the door, pull it open. Moonshine engulfs me

Us. Engulfs me us me

Moonshine—and then darkness. . . .

He was standing in the guest-house doorway.

He could not seem to remember walking here, he could not seem to remember opening the door; he was simply standing in the doorway, blinking away a wetness that dimmed his vision. In his mind there was upheaval, as though he were just starting to emerge from some sort of dreamlike state. Malignant pain in his head, too. Perspiration encasing his body, warm and mucilaginous like that caused by high fever.

Fuzzy thoughts: What's happening to me? I was all right a little while ago, I didn't feel sick—

And he saw the body.

His vision cleared and he saw the body of Maxwell Harper lying bloody and twisted on the cottage floor.

Shock. Horror. The pain in his head magnifying, manufacturing the illusion of sound in his ears, like the whine of a high-speed drill. Upheaval filling all the spaces of him; pieces of his mind seeming to fragment, cohesive thought, all rationality breaking up into a swirl of bright shards.

Look at his head, Maxwell's head, no accident somebody killed him murdered him Justice was right, psychopath killing people Briggs and Wexford it's true, but who, why does my head ache like this why can't I remember, psychopath, no, psychopath ...

Vertigo assailed him and he leaned hard against the doorjamb to keep from falling, clung to the wood there with his right hand. The hand was up in front of his face and he saw it like a claw, a fat white claw with dark spots on it, liver spots, and something else too, something adhering in the skin ridges on the backs of his knuckles, something that might have been dirt and might have been coagulated fluid, blood—blood! He ripped the hand down, thrust it behind him to hide it from his eyes, to hide it from—

—the other eyes. *There were other eyes close by, eyes that watched him in the night.*

He jerked his head up in panic. In the room's north wall, beyond Harper's body, was another window, and the shades were not drawn across it, and a face peered in at him there. Frozen behind glass, eyes enormous, mouth open with incredulity. Familiar, agonized, accusing.

Justice's face.

The implacable face of Justice.

The panic consumed him and he turned, Nicholas Augustine turned, the President of the United States turned and fled into the night.

Sixteen

Continuing his vigil, Justice had moved past the dark
tennis courts, come back through the fruit trees that grew in
even rows between the rear of the guest cottages and the
security fence. The two northernmost cottages had been
dark, but lights still shone inside the third; he had walked
up alongside it, as he had done earlier, and glanced through
the side window: Frank Tanaguchi still seated at the desk in
the front room, working over a stack of papers, listening to
classical music on a portable radio.

Justice had turned away immediately, gone past the
fourth and fifth cottages, both of which were dark, and
approached the sixth, the one occupied by Maxwell Harper.
The bright rectangle of light that was the side window drew
him again. He looked inside.

And went rigid.

And stared with sick fascination at Harper's body lying
on the floor and the President standing in the doorway
beyond, holding onto the jamb and gazing fixedly at his
right hand.

Oh my God I knew it, it's my fault, I should have found a way to prevent it—

The President, what is the President doing here?

Augustine looked ghastly; his face had a gray ravaged appearance, like decaying wood. Shock, that was it. He had come to talk to Harper for some reason and found him like this. But then why was he staring at his hand that way? It was almost as if—

No.

Chills on Justice's body, nausea in his stomach.

The President?

No! Potential *victim*, he couldn't be the psychopath!

Augustine pulled his hand down from the doorjamb, shoved it behind him. Then his expression changed all at once to one of panic and his head came up and he was looking straight across at the window. His body tensed, and Justice thought: he sees me, he'll beckon me inside now, he—

The President spun and ran.

Justice was stunned. It *couldn't* be Augustine—but when someone ran from the scene of a crime, ran from the presence of an officer of the law, it was almost always because of guilt. The President had no reason to run from his bodyguard unless he was guilty. But he couldn't be guilty.

Then why did he run?

Justice shook himself, and the policeman in him took command and sent him racing around to the front of the cottage. He slowed near the door, scanned the moonlit grounds with quick jerks of his head. At first he did not see Augustine; then there was a flash of movement to the south, in the shadows cast by a line of four-foot high cinquefoil shrubs. A second later the President appeared as a silhouette against the bright moonglow, running southeast in long lurching strides.

Justice sprinted in that direction, leaving the paths where they meandered around trees and shrubs and flowers so that he could maintain a straight-ahead course in Augustine's wake. He lost sight of him in the small copse of evergreens planted as a windbreak near the garage barns. Plunged through the trees and saw him again seventy yards away, heading across open ground toward the rear of the barns. Except for the two of them, the night seemed deserted—nothing moving anywhere. And Justice was thankful for that: he did not want anyone to see the President running, he did not want anyone else to catch him.

Catch him, he thought, catch the President.

Draw his gun and shout at him to halt, as he would have done with any homicide suspect? Hold him at bay, spread him out and search him? Question him, demand to know why he had run? A feeling of surreality came over Justice. That was the *President* up there, he was chasing the Chief Executive of the United States across the grounds of his own estate. There was a psychopath loose at The Hollows and he was running after the President and the President was not the one, he was not the one.

Ahead, Augustine had vanished again behind the first of the barns. Justice fought to lengthen his strides, reached the corner, turned past it. The President was midway along the rear wall of the second barn, running with his head down and his arms pumping like cylinder valves. The distance between them was still at least seventy-five yards.

When Augustine was beyond the second barn he veered at an angle to the west. Justice, coming out along there moments later, saw him heading toward the far side of the stable, and clenched his teeth in frustration because the gap that separated them seemed to have increased: the President was maintaining the frenzied pace of someone half his age.

The stable loomed blackly; the fence rails enclosing the corral and the paddock were like black bars drawn on a yellow-white backdrop. Augustine went past the building, along the paddock fence—but there was nothing beyond the end of it except another copse of evergreens and then the security fence. Where is he going? Justice thought. Where is he running to?

Why is he running?

Why am I running? Augustine thought.

But it was fragmented, submerged with other thought shards in the raw fluid of panic. Blood on my hand, but it isn't blood. Get away, get away from Justice, don't let him catch you. Ashtray on the floor, blood on that too, bludgeoned Maxwell to death with an ashtray. Get away. I couldn't do a thing like that. He was in love with Claire but I couldn't do a thing like that. Psychopath. Three murders, I should have listened to Justice. Christopher, I didn't do it. Run. Help me, I don't know what's happening to me. Run!

And his brain continued to give motor commands and his body continued to respond: flight, escape. The exertion constricted his chest, formed a stitch in his left side; he could not get enough air into his lungs. Sweat streamed into his eyes, made perception of his surroundings an aqueous blur, as though he were running at great speed underwater.

He did not quite know where he was until his foot stubbed against something and he staggered off-balance, nearly fell, then caught blindly onto a round vertical object and held himself upright. The familiar rough-wood feel of the object transmitted to his mind and became the words *fence post,* and when he dragged an arm up to clear his eyes he saw he was at the far corner of the paddock. Run. I didn't do anything. Justice is after you, run!

The horses.

Yes, yes, the horses. Not even Justice can run as fast as a horse.

Augustine shoved away from the fence post and ran along the far side of the paddock. He reached the stable without seeing Justice, his breath coming now in small explosive grunts. The door to the tack room was on that side of the building, closed now but never locked, and it opened under his hand. He went inside, shut the door after him.

Familiar odors: manure from the adjacent stalls, good oiled leather, liniment and hay and the gamy effluvium of horses. Without pausing—he knew the tack room even in darkness—he went to the door that led to the stalls, swung it open. Turned back, took a bridle off its wall peg, dragged one of the heavy saddles down and struggled with it into the stalls.

Some of the horses had begun to move restlessly; one of them made a soft blowing sound. Casey Jones was in the third stall, where he was always kept, and Augustine went there and opened the half-door and took the saddle inside. Casey nickered but stood still: obedient and trusting, a fine old engineer. Augustine threw the saddle on the animal's back, cinched the straps, hooked the bridle on. Hurry, Justice is outside—and he caught the reins and led Casey Jones out of the stall, across to the double doors in the west wall. I didn't do it—and he mounted the bay and then leaned down to unlatch the doors.

I don't know why I'm doing this—and he shoved the doors wide and heard himself say "Run!" and dug his heels into Casey Jones's flanks.

Justice was in the trees beyond the paddock, searching frantically for the President, when the night erupted in sound: a sharp wooden clattering, what might have been a cry, the unexpected pound of a horse's hooves.

He wheeled around, ran back toward the paddock. And to the north of the stable the horse and rider—Augustine, it could only be Augustine—came galloping into view, heading toward the east gate. Justice stopped, made an involuntary sound of his own that was almost a sob. Why? he thought. If he's not guilty, *why?*

Then he began to run for the tack room.

*   *   *

The guard on the north gate came hurrying out of the small gatehouse as Augustine neck-reined Casey Jones to a halt. He stared open-mouthed and said, "Mr. President! What—"

"Open the gate," Augustine shouted at him.

"But it's almost nine o'clock, sir. You can't go out riding alone at this time of—"

"Open the gate!" Stop me, don't let me go. "That's a direct order, mister. Open this goddamn gate!"

The guard hesitated, frowning, uncertain. And then nodded and said, "Yes sir, if you say so," and went back into the gatehouse. A moment later the gate began electronically to swing open.

Augustine waited only until the opening was large enough for the horse to pass through; then he kicked Casey Jones again and sent him charging out onto the moonlit meadowland beyond.

Justice knew something about horses—he had taken riding lessons at one of the academies in Maryland during a long-ago summer—but he had little experience with outfitting one of the animals. Even though he had put on the stable lights, it took him long agonizing minutes to get the saddle and bridle into place on a small roan mare.

Can't let him get away. Innocent or guilty I've got to stop him. . . .

He swung finally into the saddle, heeled the mare through the stable doors and round the north side of the building and straight toward the east gate. The night was still quiet, empty; all this running, afoot and now on horseback, the noise and the tension like static electricity on the cool night air, and no one had been alerted. It was as if the world had diminished to a microcosm in which only the two of them had significance, in which only he and the President struggled toward truth and sanity.

When he neared the gate he saw that it still stood open, saw the guard standing there looking bewilderedly through it to the northeast. At the sound of the mare's hoofbeats the guard turned, brought his legs and his boots together and raised one arm—an awkward request to stop that seemed more like a parody of a Nazi salute. But Justice slowed the mare only long enough to shout at him, "It's all right, I'll handle it, I'll handle it," and then he was past him and through the gate.

More than a hundred yards distant, silhouetted against the clear sky, he could see the black joined shapes of man and horse. He slapped the mare's neck with the reins, pounded his heels into the animal's sides, and went after the fleeing figure of the President as if it were life itself pelting away from him.

Seventeen

The wind whipped coldly at Augustine's face, billowed his hair and Casey Jones's mane, burned like ice on his bare fingers clutching the reins. But the wind was an ally, the wind and the night and the mountains and the horse. He was part of it, part of them all, and together they offered him freedom.

From what? From what?

The smells of dust and pine and horse sweat assailed his nostrils; the staccato beat of the bay's hooves was like thunder in his ears. His heart skittered wildly. The sensation of speed was almost exhilarating: moon-drenched meadowland flashing past them, forest slopes rushing closer and beckoning sanctuary. Oh yes, he was in his element now; Justice couldn't catch him now.

I want him to catch me, I didn't do anything.

He twisted his head to look over his shoulder. And Justice was there, just coming through the gate on one of the smaller horses, coming after him. One-man posse. Relentless. Justice on the prod.

Augustine pulled his head around again, into the wind.

When the mare stretched out into full gallop Justice clung to the reins with one hand and to the saddle horn with the other; he had never ridden at this speed before; he was afraid of being jarred out of the saddle. More than a hundred yards still separated him from the President, and there were less than a hundred yards between Augustine and the northeast slope. The horse he was riding was Casey Jones, and Casey was bigger and faster than the mare: Justice knew there was no hope of catching up to him before he reached the trees.

And what would he do once he was into them? The trail forked halfway up the slope, Justice remembered; the main path went up along the river gorge to Lookout Point, and the branch hooked back to the south and eventually wound down again to the meadowland. There were no other trails up there—but the President was an expert horseman, he would probably be able to break a path through the trees if he chose to. And yet even then he would have nowhere to go. You couldn't get from the ridge into the rangeland valleys farther east because of high rock walls and impassable undergrowth; the slope was a kind of mountain cul-de-sac.

Should he draw his gun, fire a warning shot? Surreality again. Law officer chasing a desperado on horseback, a scene from a thousand Western movies; only the desperado was the President, he could not fire a shot in pursuit of the President—

A new thought struck Justice: Suppose I catch him and he refuses to give up? Suppose he tries to fight me, forces me to use my weapon? No. I couldn't do it. Even if he's guilty, even in self-defense and the performance of my duty, I couldn't shoot him.

How could I shoot the President of the United States?

At the base of the slope, where the trail began its climb into the trees, Augustine automatically slowed Casey Jones and gave the animal his head, letting him make the transition from level to ascending ground at a safe pace of his own. The horse surged upward, snorting, chest heaving. Augustine tightened the reins again then, used his heels— and they were into the woods, darkness and shadow closed around them and the moonshine was gone except for random beams glowing like spotlights on the forest floor.

Into the woods, but not out of the woods. We're not out of the woods yet.

It was hushed in there, so still that the muffled rhythm of Casey Jones's hooves seemed to echo from tree trunk to tree trunk: dull hollow axlike thuds. Low-hanging branches seemed to reach for him as he sped past; he saw them as fingers, the groping fingers of Justice, and ducked his head and flattened his body forward to avoid them, resting his cheek on the wet leather that had formed on the horse's neck. Receding below, the trail appeared to him then as a tunnel, long and dark and unfamiliar, alien, leading him— where? Where?

For God's sake help me.

He closed his eyes, but as soon as he did that he saw the blood residue on his hand, saw Harper's shattered skull. He popped them open again, and they were wet with sweat—or was it tears? No. A President does not weep; he must never weep. Not even to mourn his dead. Not even to mourn himself.

The trail fork loomed ahead, but he did not slow Casey Jones this time, had no impulse at all to veer off onto the branch path. Lookout Point, that was where he was head-

ing. Not by choice, by happenstance. Wasn't it? Lookout
Point. I was up there yesterday with Maxwell, but Maxwell
is dead; somebody murdered him, but it wasn't me. Lookout
Point. High ground, the high place.

Why?

And there was bright moonlight ahead, and the trail
began to curve out of the trees to parallel the rim of the
gorge, and he heard the low rumbling voice of the river.
Like a train, it sounded like a train. Faster! He kicked at
Casey Jones's lathered flanks, sent the animal through the
curve to where he could see the high ground above. The
horse began to balk, laboring near exhaustion. Don't quit on
me now, old engineer, we're almost there, almost up the
mountain. He held Casey's head steady, heeled his flanks
again, and they went up, up—out at last onto the grassy flat
of Lookout Point.

Augustine reined the bay to a panting halt in the center
of it, raised up until he was standing in the stirrups. The
redwoods and the pines rose all around like guardians, and
the high granite wall shone as smooth as marble in the
moonlight, and far beyond the gorge the ridges and valleys
glistened black and gold, and the ghosts of the vanished
castle were grazing there, and the tips of the mountains
pierced the sky and impaled clusters of stars. Splendor,
symmetry, enormity. Such a long time since he had seen it
like this; years, fifteen years, sitting up here with Claire on a
summer night fifteen years ago, shedding their clothes and
making love on the soft grass—

Claire.

A shudder ran through him. She'll be sick when she finds
out, she'll hate me. Protect her from it, don't let her find
out. But it's too late. Justice will tell her, implacable Justice.
Oh Claire, I didn't do it, I'm not a psychopath. Am I?
Claire?

He swung out of the saddle and walked slowly toward the

gorge. Beauty—and ugliness. Peace and chaos, life and death, sanity and madness. I wanted beauty like this for the world, and love and peace for the world, and instead I gave disruption and death. Only I didn't. Only I did. I didn't give enough and I gave too much.

He stopped near the precipice; the train-voice of the river was loud, loud, like a fast freight thundering through the Big Bend tunnel on the C&O line more than a hundred years ago. He stared at the mountain in the distance. Yes, the mountain: hammerin' on the mountain and my hammer strikin' fire. They said to me We believe this mountain's sinkin' in, and I said to them Oh my, it's my hammer just a-hossin' in the wind. That's how it was in the beginning. Hammer strikin' fire on the mountain. Me and John Henry, steel-drivin' men. But not any more. Hammer striking men now—Briggs and Julius and Maxwell. Hammer striking flesh and bone.

The train-voice seemed to be calling to him. He moved still closer to the gorge, to where he could look straight down at the black water below. Rushing, rushing, old fast freight heading down the mountain, heading home. Heading home. Just too much hammerin', that's all. I drove so hard my poor heart broke. And I laid down my hammer and I—

Is that the answer?

I laid down my hammer and I died, Lawd, Lawd.

Yes. Heading home.

I laid down my hammer and I died.

Augustine took another step. And stood on the brink.

Justice was twenty yards from Lookout Point when the President came into his line of sight: standing at the very edge of the river gorge and leaning forward as if . . . Jesus, as if he were about to jump. Panic sliced at him; he rein-slapped the mare, opened his mouth and bellowed, "Mr. President! No, Mr. President!"

Augustine seemed to go rigid, then to hunch forward even farther. But he did not move his feet, just kept on standing there, poised, as Justice battled the weary mare up onto the flat and flung himself to the ground. He thought of rushing across the thirty yards that separated them, grabbing the President and pulling him back; only the sudden aggression might startle him enough to send him toppling over the edge. Justice held his position, tension cording the muscles in his neck and back, the acidlike nausea eating away again at the walls of his stomach.

"Mr. President," he said, forcing calm and reason into his voice, "come away from there so we can talk."

Augustine was silent. His body appeared to oscillate, as if it were racked with a series of tremors.

Desperation clawed at Justice. He had to move; he couldn't just stand there. He took a long cautious step forward and to his right, so that he was directly behind the President. Another step, watching the ground to keep from putting his foot down on something brittle. A third. A fourth. Twenty-five yards between them. A fifth step—

Abruptly, without turning, Augustine said, "Go away, Justice. Leave me alone."

Justice hesitated. The agony in those words scraped like sandpaper across his nerves. "I can't do that, sir," he said thickly. "You know I can't."

Another step.

Another.

"I'm so tired," Augustine said. "I can't hammer anymore."

Another step. Twenty yards.

"Let me help you, Mr. President. I can help you if you'll—"

And Augustine pivoted, a graceless one-hundred-and-eighty-degree turn without stepping away from the edge. Justice came to a standstill, pulse racing—but the President only stood looking at him, fingers clasped in front of him

now as if in an attitude of prayer. Justice bit his lip to keep
it from trembling; bit it hard enough to draw the salty taste
of blood.

"I wouldn't hurt you, sir," he said, "you know that. I only
want to help—"

"Nobody can help me. It's time to head home."

Keep him talking! "Why did you run, sir? That's all I
want to know, that's the only reason I came after you."

"You think I'm a murderer."

"No sir. I just want to know why you ran."

"I was afraid. I'm sick, Christopher."

"I'll take you to a doctor—"

"It's too late for that. But I didn't do it, I didn't kill them.
Tell Claire that, tell them all."

Justice stretched out his hand palm up, imploring. "Take
my hand, sir—"

"I didn't do it, Christopher," the President said.

And unclasped his fingers and jumped backward into the
gorge.

"I didn't do it, Christopher," Augustine said, and unclasped his fingers and jumped backward into the gorge, and
the instant he became airborne and weightless, falling, he
felt the terror and the upheaval leave him and he thought: I
didn't do it, I really *didn't* do it! and because he was
innocent and because he did not have to hammer anymore a
kind of wild soaring joy, not unlike that of orgasm, came
into him. No more pain, no more responsibility, no more
pressure, just these few moments of soaring and then he
would join the river train below and it would carry him
down the mountain and carry him home; soaring and
falling and
   impact
   and free.

                    *   *   *

Justice watched in horror as the President jumped, disappeared beyond the rim. He heard himself shout something and threw his body forward, onto his knees, onto his belly, and crawled to the edge and shoved his head out and looked down.

In time to see Augustine's body turn over and over between the jagged black walls, a speck plummeting through moonlight and darkness, and strike an outcropping of granite with a sound that carried faintly up to Justice, like an echo of death, and fall again and finally vanish into the river.

He wanted to cry, to scream, to tear things with his hands; instead he pulled himself back and lay with his head cradled in his arms. Self-condemnation: I should have saved him, I should have saved him! Then there was grief, black and consuming. And then, after a long while, there was nothing at all—as though the defensive machinery of his mind had erected a wall to block off emotion.

I didn't do it, Christopher.

The President's last words. And they began to repeat themselves inside his head, slowly, steadily, like a liturgical chant. But he did do it, Justice thought. The denial had been a cry for relief, relief of guilt: he knew he was mentally ill, he couldn't cope with his psychosis, and in the end the knowledge had become so intolerable that it had forced him into taking his own life.

I didn't do it, Christopher.

Unbalanced, yes, no question of that—but suppose it wasn't psychosis after all? Suppose it was a complete but nonviolent breakdown brought about by the enormous pressure and anxiety of the past few days? Suppose the shock of finding Harper's body had unbalanced him so severely that he had half-believed he was guilty, run because of that? Suppose he had committed suicide *only* because he was sick and frightened?

I didn't do it, Christopher.

Justice sat up; he was cold, cold—and there were thoughts beginning to move dimly at the edges of his mind, as though trying to form some sort of visceral insight. He got to his feet, started over to where the horses were nuzzling grass in the moonlight. Stopped again and stared sightlessly at the black line of trees to the south.

I didn't do it, Christopher.

Then who did? If it wasn't the President, who *is* it?

The insight began to come together.

I didn't do it, Christopher.

And he knew who it was.

Insight, intuition—just like that he knew who the psychopath was and it was not the President; it was not the President, he had died for nothing.

Justice ran to the roan mare and swung up into the saddle, heeled the horse swiftly downslope.

Toward the person who had murdered not three men but four; toward the person who had murdered Nicholas Augustine.

Eighteen

The front door of the house was unlocked, and Justice opened it without knocking and stepped inside. A ceiling globe burned in the hallway and flickers of firelight created dancing shadows in the family room; everywhere else there was darkness. He paused for a moment, listening to the purring and the snapping of flames, and then slowly walked to the doorway on his left and entered the family room.

She was sitting on the couch near the hearth, hands folded in her lap, head turned toward him. Claire Augustine: the First Lady, the President's wife.

Murderer.

Justice hesitated again. How many times had he read scenes just like this in mystery novels? The detective, the policeman, facing the murderer in the final chapter; the confrontation scene in which the truth was revealed at last: the motives, the hidden relationships, the intricacies of plot and counterplot. The clues and the clever deductions. The confession. The wrap-up.

But this was not a mystery novel and this was not that kind of confrontation. What was involved here was real crime and real pain, the real deaths of the attorney general and the domestic affairs advisor and the press secretary and the President of the United States—murder and madness so devastating that it literally affected the lives and futures of hundreds of millions of people throughout the world. This was the confrontation at the end of the greatest single tragedy in the history of America, and it was awesome, and it belonged with terrible irony to him and to the woman sitting across the room.

Justice went to stand in front of her. And felt nothing in that moment except emotional exhaustion—no anger, no hatred, no pity, not even grief. If there was anything left in him at all, it was a sense of shame.

"Mrs. Augustine," he said.

She seemed to quail at the sound of his voice, the grim authority in it. She looked small sitting there, hunched, as if she had withdrawn into herself so deeply that it had become physical as well as mental. Her eyes were wide, but there was no lustre in them, no animation—the eyes of an interloper inhabiting the body of the First Lady.

He said tonelessly, "The President is dead, Mrs. Augustine."

Her reaction was convulsive; a look of fearful disbelief made her face seem grotesque in the flickers of orange light. Her hands came up, fluttering like white wings, and turned palms outward as if to push away the truth of his words. She whispered. "What are you *saying?*" in a voice that trembled, nearly broke.

"It's true," Justice said. "He fell into the river gorge at Lookout Point. I was there but I couldn't save him. I just couldn't save him."

"Oh my God!"

"He thought he'd killed Mr. Harper," Justice said. "He was a sick man and he found Harper dead in his cottage and he thought he'd done it. But he didn't do it, Mrs. Augustine. We both know that."

"No," she said, "no," and tears welled in her eyes, began to spill over her cheeks in glistening runnels. Her body quivered, her hands came together above her breast and wrapped in the material of her blouse, twisted it so hard Justice heard a faint ripping sound.

He forced himself to keep looking at her. "It was you, Mrs. Augustine," he said. "You're the one who killed Harper and Briggs and Wexford, you're the one who's really ill. And you killed the President too, just as sure as if you'd bludgeoned him to death like the others."

"Stop it! Please stop it ..."

"I don't know why you did it," Justice said. "Maybe you thought you were helping the President, saving his career by eliminating people you believed were his enemies—"

"I can't stand any more of this, I can't take any more!"

"Then confess the truth and it will be over."

She stared up at him with her huge wet eyes. And the tears stopped and the trembling stopped, and he could almost see her gathering herself together at the edges. "Yes," she said finally, in a voice that was dull and lifeless, but controlled now, "the truth. It's time for the truth; it's much too late for anything else."

"That's right," Justice said. "Go ahead, Mrs. Augustine."

"I waited too long," she said. She was not looking at him now, was looking instead into the fire. "Out of love, out of blind hope. Out of weakness. I've always thought I was strong, but I'm not; it was just a facade. I didn't know what to do; I tried to confide in Elizabeth Miller, of all people, but I couldn't bring myself to do it. I was like a little girl alone in the woods at night, surrounded by shadows I couldn't understand and couldn't cope with. I kept thinking the night would end and they would all go away. God forgive me, I waited too long."

Justice frowned. "I don't have any idea what you're

talking about, ma'am. Why don't you just confess the truth and be done with it?"

"I am confessing the truth. I'm doing what I should have done days ago, weeks ago."

This isn't going the way it should, he thought. Not the last chapter of a mystery novel but a confrontation nevertheless, and it isn't going the way it should. It was as if she had managed to take subtle command of it, as if their roles had somehow shifted.

"I'll ask you again," he said. "Why did you kill Maxwell Harper? Why did you kill the press secretary and the attorney general?"

"I didn't kill them," she said. "No one killed them."

"What?"

"They are not dead."

He gaped at her. "What kind of a lie is that? Of course they're dead!"

Her eyes on him again, tears in them. "Austin Briggs is alive in Washington. And so is Julius Wexford; he got off the train with us yesterday, he took a car from the station to San Francisco."

All wrong, this is all wrong. "I don't know what you're trying to do, Mrs. Augustine, but it won't work. Briggs and Wexford are dead. And Harper is dead, he's lying out in his cottage right now with his skull crushed. If you make me do it I'll take you out there and show him to you."

"No," she said, "you won't."

"Why won't I?"

"Because he isn't there. He was never there."

"He's *there—*"

"He doesn't exist," she said.

Confusion in him now, like a black mist. He shook his head, saw her get painfully to her feet and reach out an entreating hand to him—as he had reached out a hand to the President on Lookout Point. He backed away from her with revulsion.

"You can't keep lying to me," he said. "I'm a trained policeman—"

"You're not a policeman."

"Christopher Justice is a *policeman.*"

"Christopher Justice doesn't exist either."

Pain in his head now. "I'm standing here in front of you!"

"Nicholas Augustine is standing in front of me. *You are Nicholas Augustine.*"

And the mist, the mist. "The President is dead! I saw him die on Lookout Point, I couldn't save him!"

"You haven't left this house tonight. You've been here with me all along."

"No, no ..."

"Oh God I hate this," she said in anguish, "I hate seeing you this way, Nicholas—"

"Don't call me that, don't call me by his name."

"—but I've got to make you understand. You're the President, you're Nicholas Augustine. Maxwell Harper and Christopher Justice are imaginary people; your poor over-worked mind created them and gave them histories and functions and finally made you *become* each of them. For the past month I've listened to you speaking in their voices, different voices like the one you're using now; I've listened to you carry on two- and three-way conversations with yourself, I've heard you fantasize entire events and situations, distort other things that actually did take place, mix up fantasy and reality in your mind ..."

He retreated from her again, but she moved after him, hands clasped at her breast, and kept talking, talking, words and sentence fragments piercing his ears like needles, *terrified me from the first, I just didn't know what to do,* flames in the fireplace leaping at him, trying to grab him, *didn't happen very often until this past week and never in public, I deluded myself into believing no one suspected and we could get through until January, just until January because I thought I could convince you eventually not to run for reelection,* the mist swirling behind his eyes now, *love you so much, Nicholas, I only wanted to protect you from shame,* his back coming up against the curtains over the French doors, *never thought it would get this bad, so bad you would imagine people murdered, even your own death,* gliding along the wall beside the doors but she kept advancing with him, *then Austin called me on Wednesday and said you'd been to see him in his office, talking to him in a strange voice as if you were another person, I had to lie and tell him it was a game you were playing, only a game,* roaring in his ears like that of a train, *terrible shock when you fantasized Austin's death, all I could think of was to get you away from Washington as soon as possible,* up against the couch, around the couch, *realized Julius suspected the truth too when I talked to him on the train, and when you told me yesterday he was dead I finally found the courage to call Doctor Whiting, but he was away from the Capital and couldn't get here right away,* moving toward the hall doorway, *hate myself for telling you to fire Maxwell tonight, I should have guessed you might fantasize murdering even one of your own personas,* pain and mist, mist and pain, *accused me just now of killing all those people, killing you, I couldn't stand it, I couldn't wait, I had to tell you the truth—*

She stopped speaking, turned her head away from him toward the doorway as if reacting to a sound only she could hear. Then her shoulders slumped and she said, "Oh thank God. Thank God you're finally here."

He looked at the doorway and there was no one there.

"Nicholas," she said, "It's Walt Peterson and Doctor Whiting."

No one there. No one in the room except him and Mrs. Augustine—

Only then the ceiling lights came on and she was nowhere near the light switch, and he blinked and began to shake his head, the mist swirling, swirling, and in the center of it a small spot of truth and acceptance, and he heard himself whimper and then say, "I'm Christopher Justice, I have to call my superiors, I have to notify my superiors," and he ran for the doorway.

Hands caught him before he reached it, hands that were not there, hands that held him with invisible fingers, and he cried out and struggled desperately for a moment, just a moment before the strength went out of him and he became rag-doll limp. The hands guided him gently to a chair and sat him down, and he heard Claire Augustine saying brokenly, "Nicholas, oh Nicholas, what have we done to you, what did I do to you?" and heard another voice too—Doctor Whiting's voice?—coming to him as if from a great distance.

And a voice came out of *him* then that was not his own, a voice that belonged to the President, and the President said clearly and lucidly, "You shouldn't have let me go on, Claire. I might have done something unspeakable, didn't you realize that?"

Then the voice was still, and he put his head in his hands and wept in mourning for the President, the fall of the President, the last long fall of President Nicholas Franklin Augustine.

Then the voice is still, and we put our head in our hands and weep. But not in mourning and not for me.

We weep instead for what might have been, for what could have been done about Briggs and Wexford and Kineen and Oberdorfer and the media and the minority party and the Indians and the National Committee and the pressure groups and the electorate and Israel and the Arabs and the Russians and the Red Chinese. We have known from the beginning that death is the only answer; and there is no moonshine in our soul. If only we had carried that knowledge to its ultimate conclusion. If only we had thought of it.

We could *really* have committed an act of mercy then.

We could have murdered them all.